RK
PRINCESS

NIDHI CHANANI

With color by
Elizabeth Kramer

VIKING

VIKING
An imprint of Penguin Random House LLC, New York

First published in the United States of America by Viking,
an imprint of Penguin Random House LLC, 2022

Visit us online at penguinrandomhouse.com.

Library of Congress Cataloging-in-Publication Data is available.

Manufactured in China

ISBN 9780593464601

1 3 5 7 9 10 8 6 4 2

TOPL

Design by Opal Roengchai
Text set in Nidhi Chanani
The illustrations were created created digitally with organic textures

For Leela,
who asked me to draw a shark princess
on her fourth birthday and inspired this series

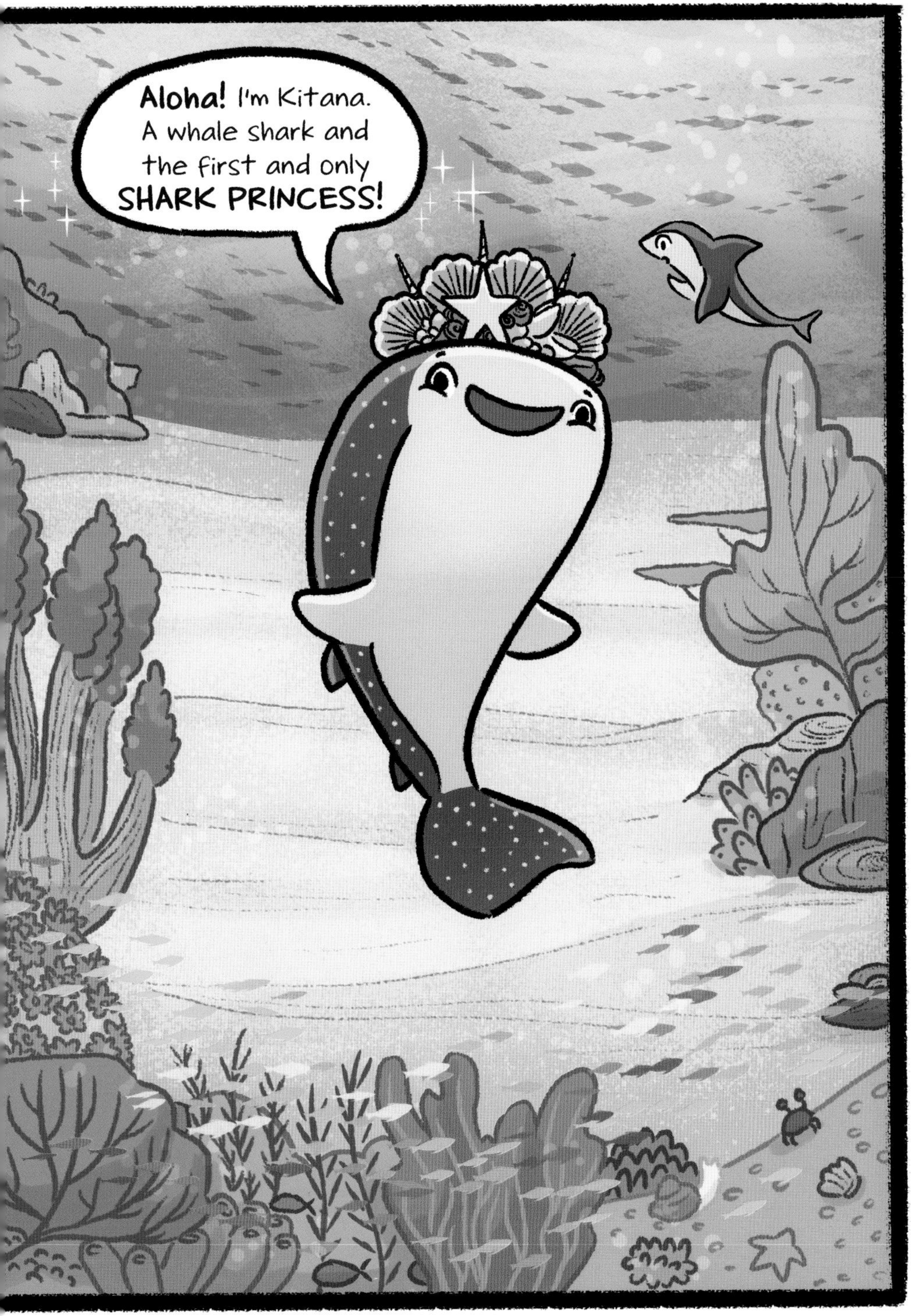
Aloha! I'm Kitana. A whale shark and the first and only **SHARK PRINCESS!**

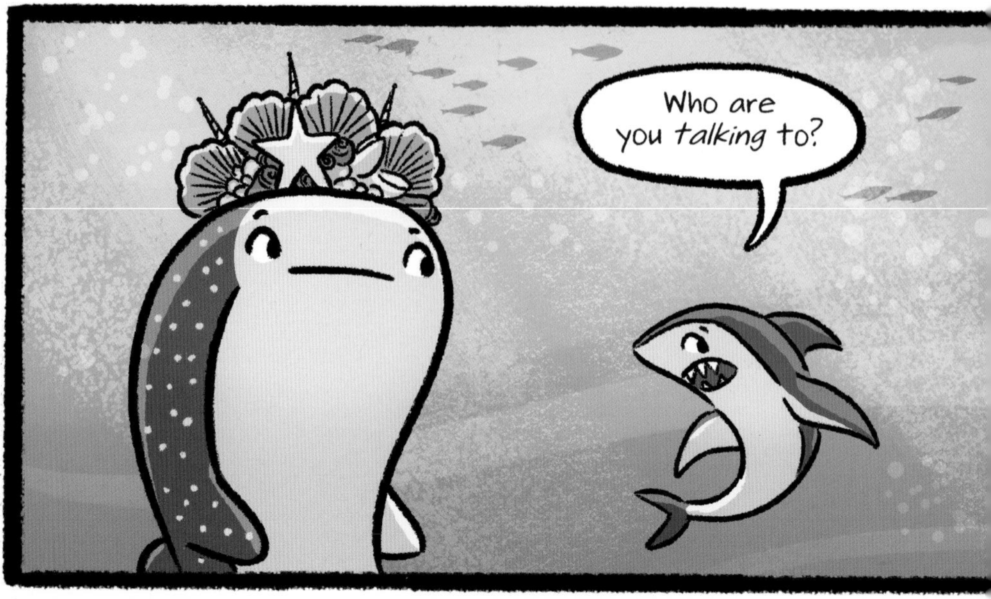
Who are you *talking* to?

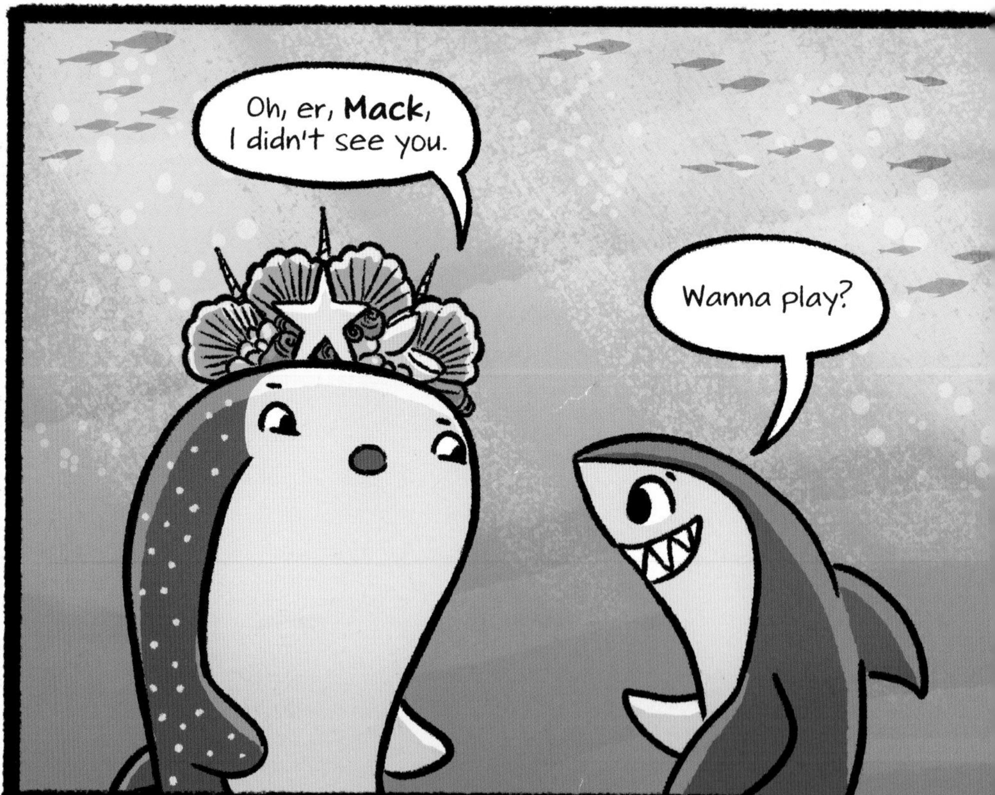
Oh, er, **Mack**, I didn't see you.
Wanna play?

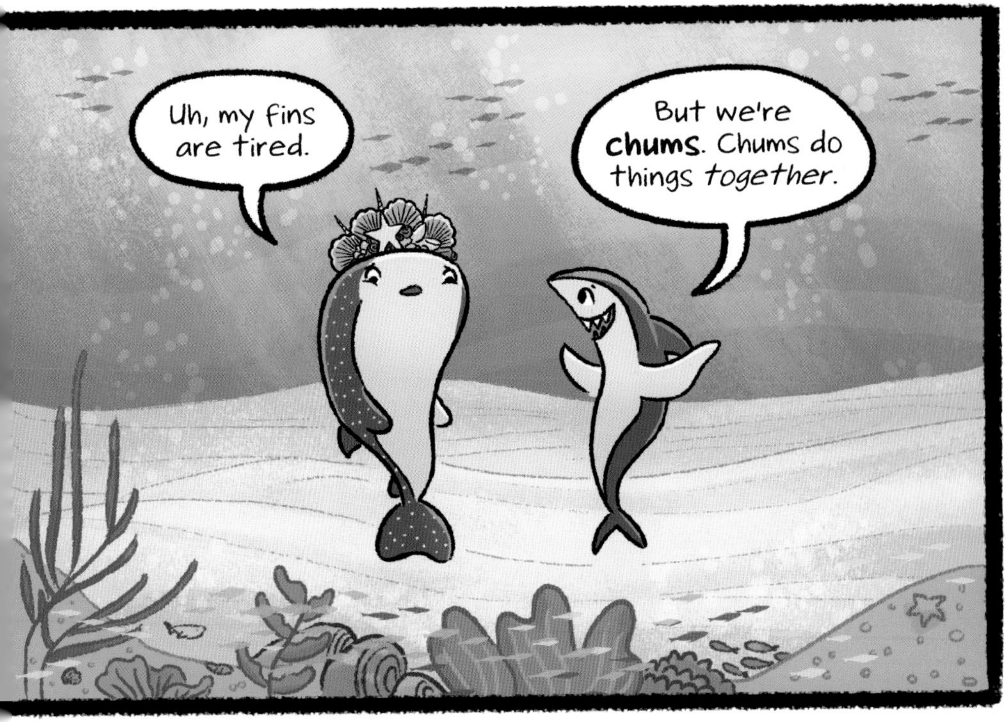
Uh, my fins are tired.
But we're **chums**. Chums do things *together*.

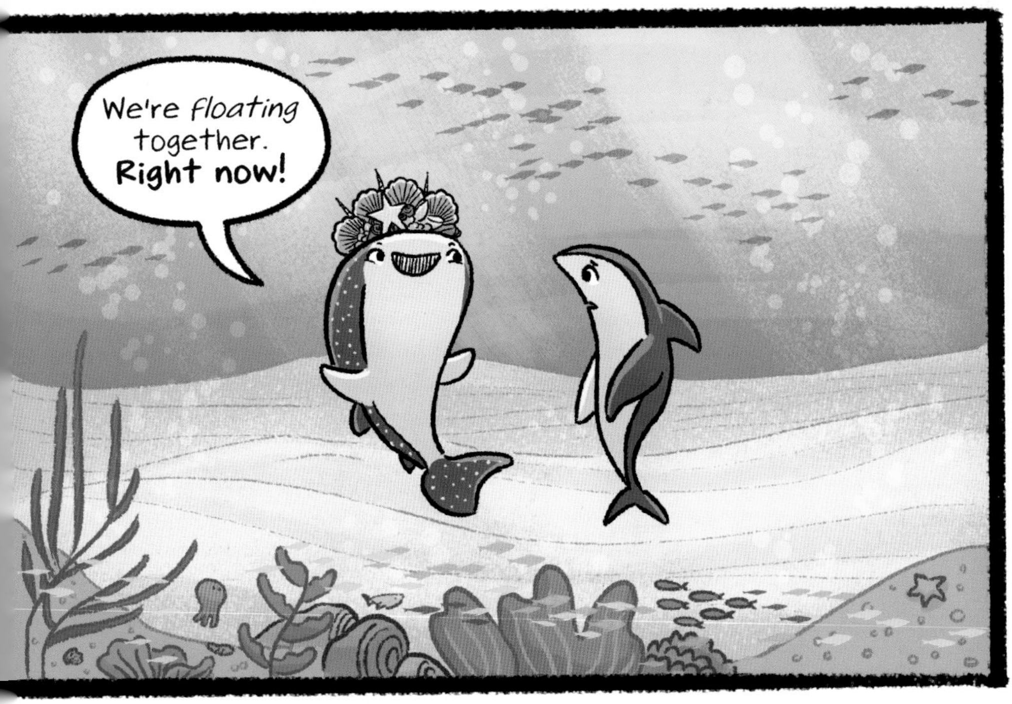
We're *floating* together. **Right now!**

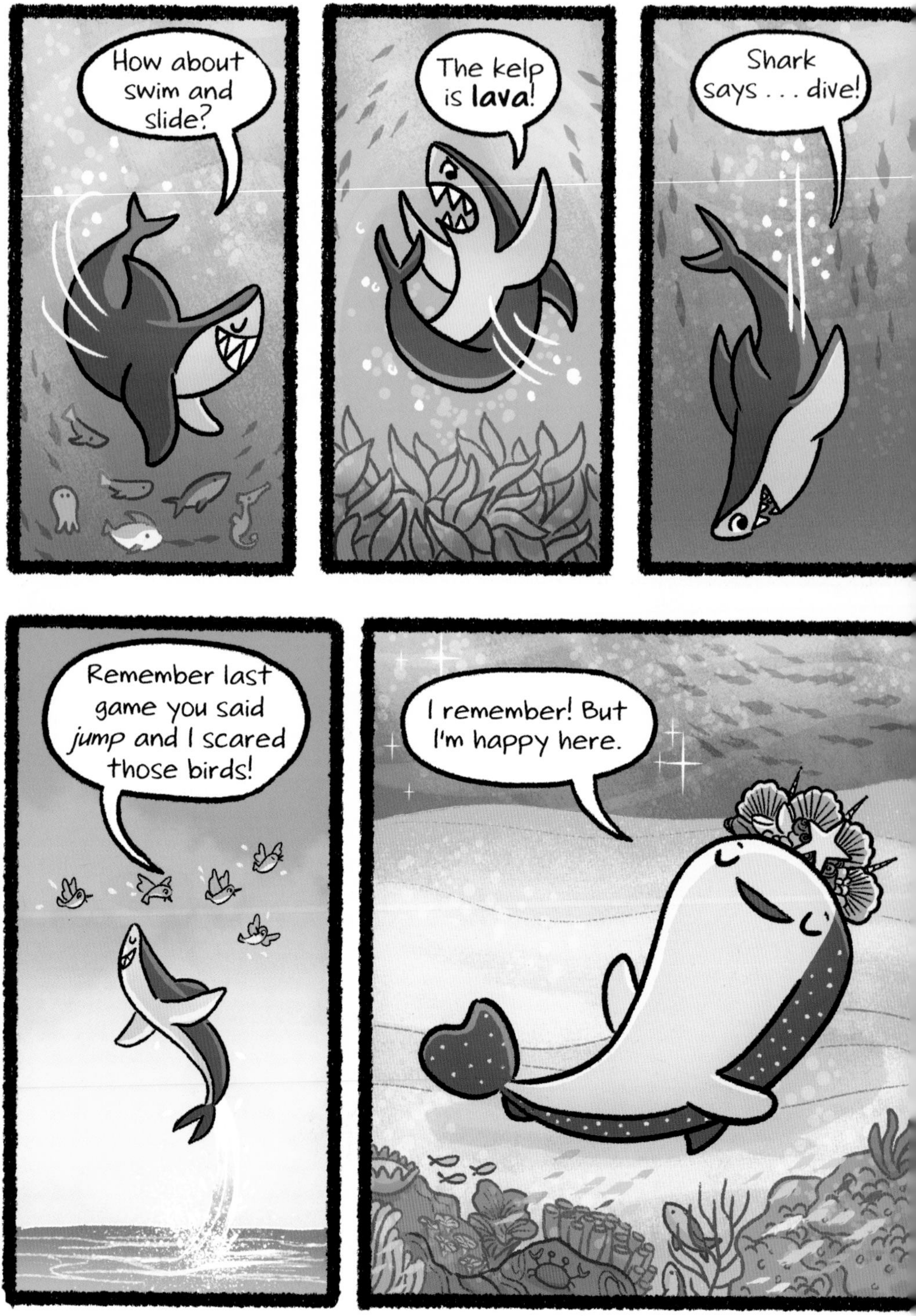
How about swim and slide?
The kelp is **lava**!
Shark says . . . dive!
Remember last game you said *jump* and I scared those birds!
I remember! But I'm happy here.

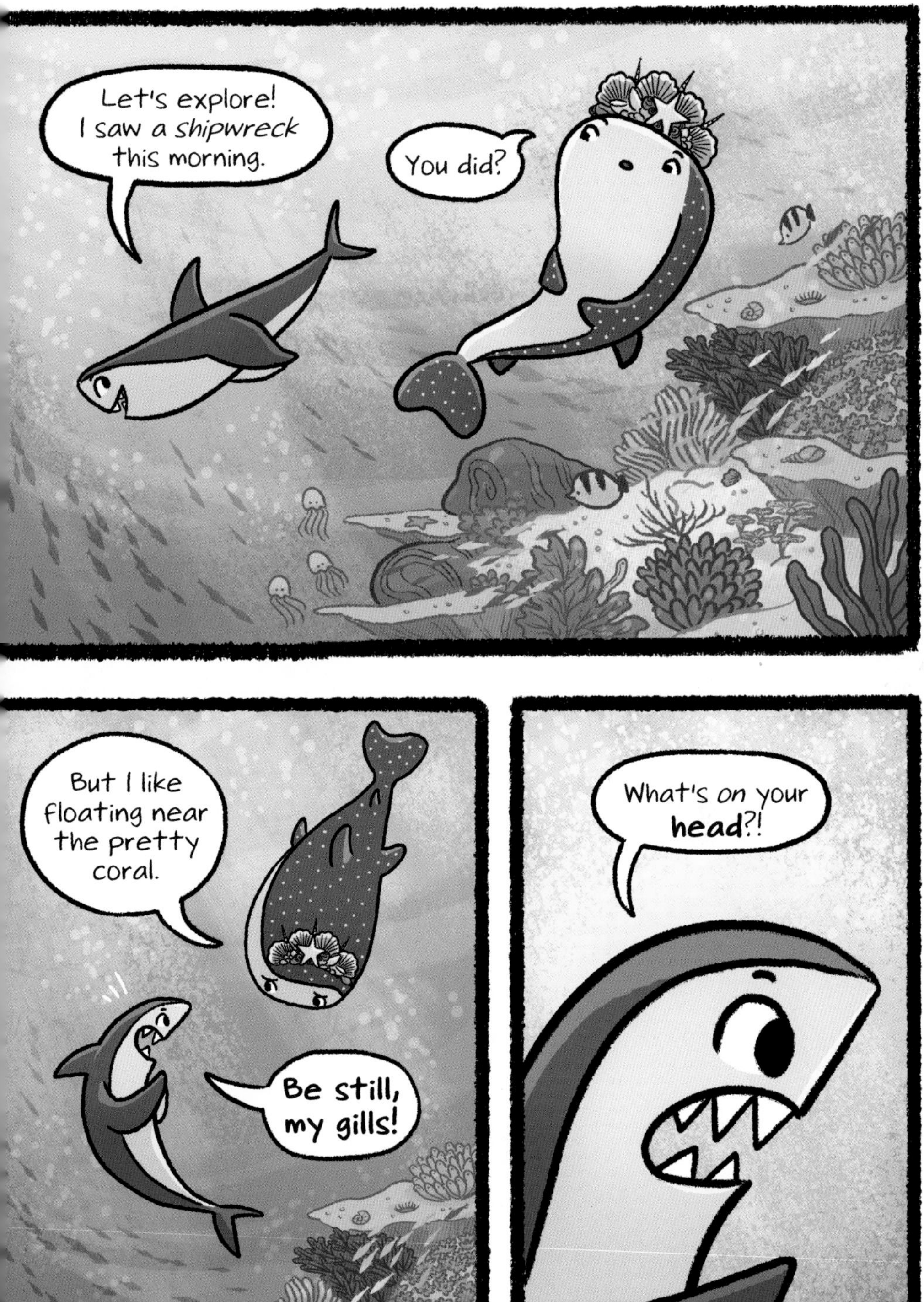
Let's explore! I saw a *shipwreck* this morning.
You did?
But I like floating near the pretty coral.
Be still, my gills!
What's on your **head**?!

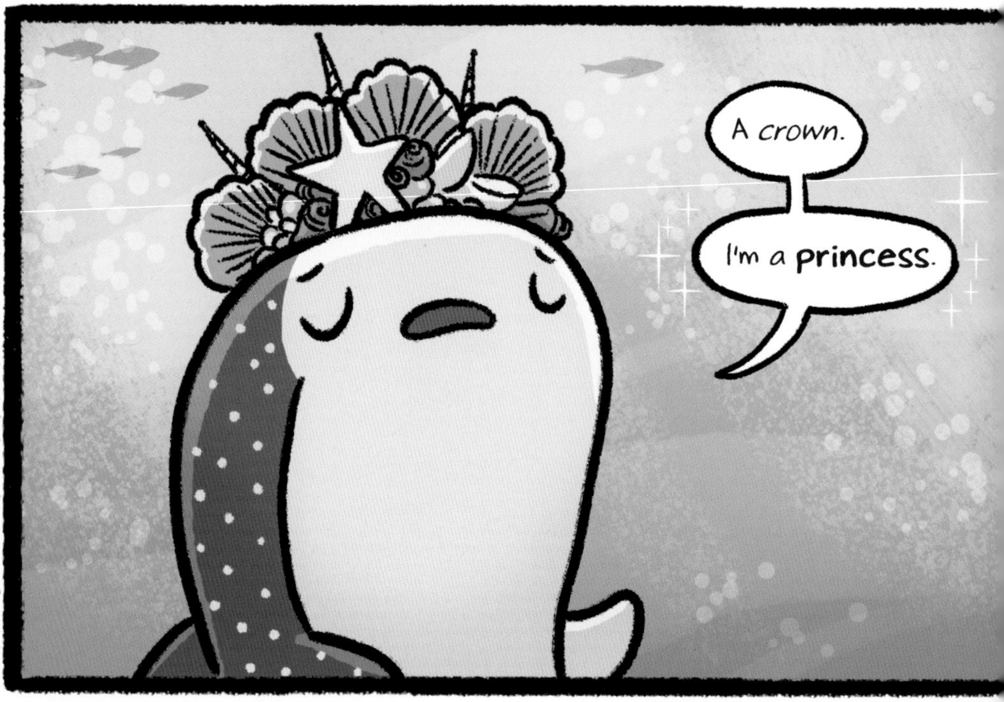
A crown.
I'm a princess.

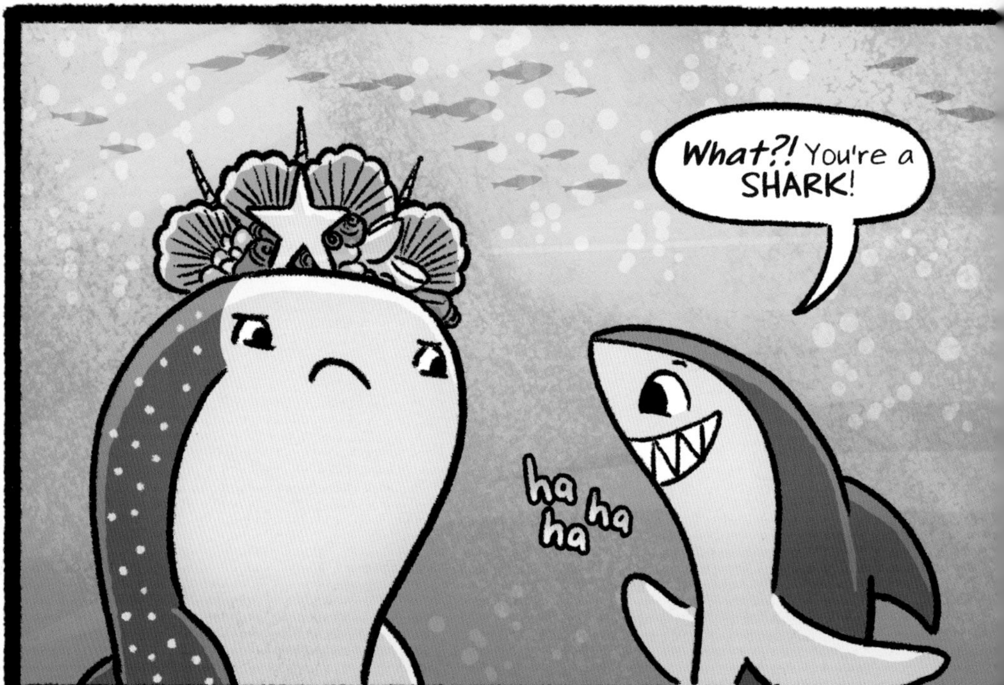
What?! You're a SHARK!
ha ha ha

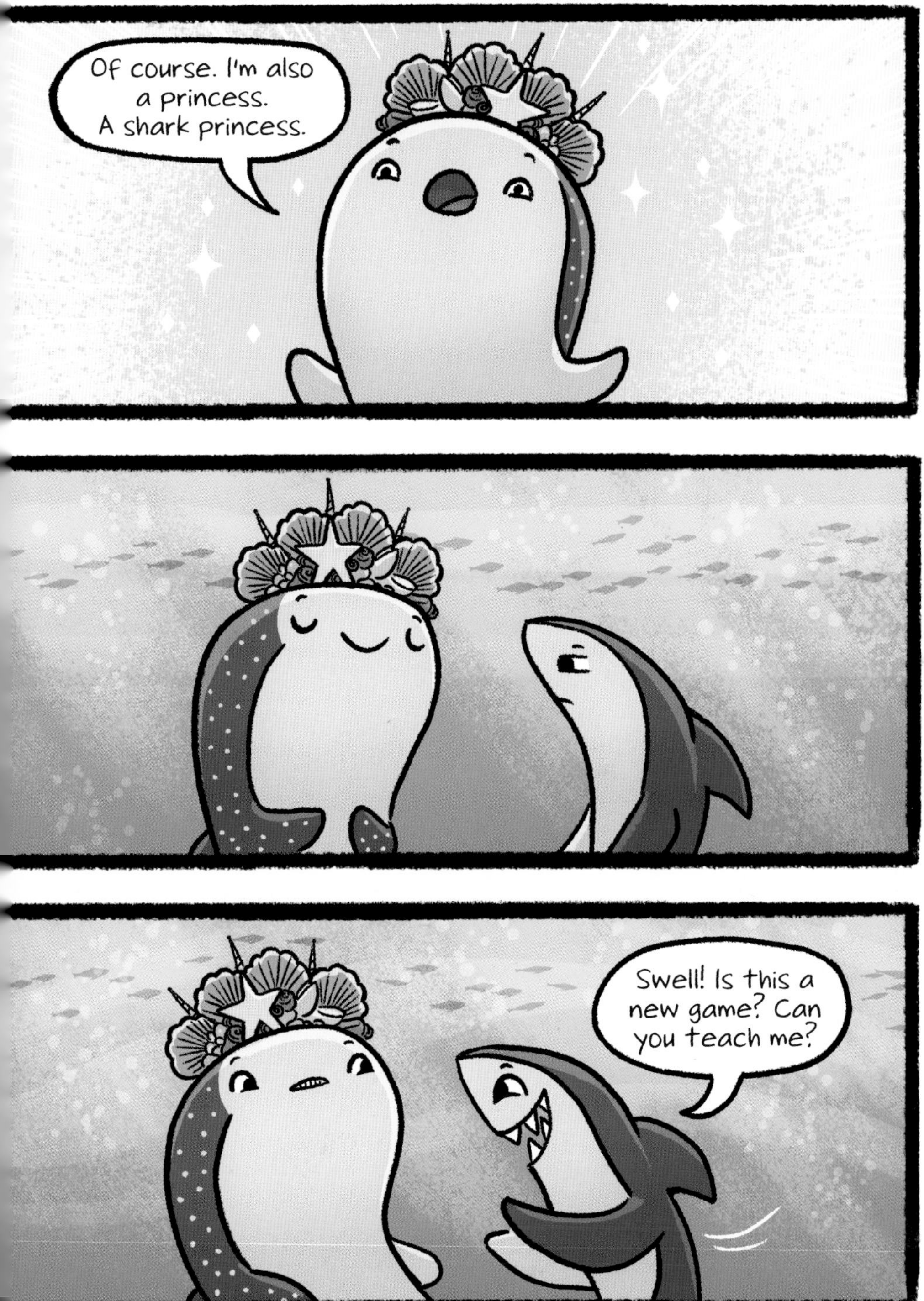
Of course. I'm also a princess. A shark princess.
Swell! Is this a new game? Can you teach me?

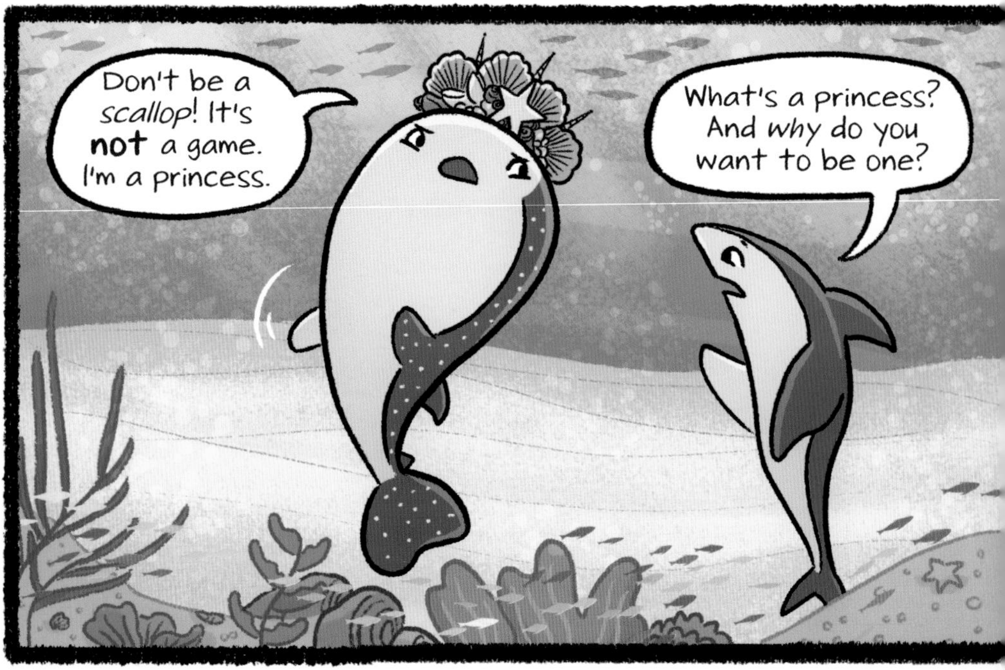
Don't be a *scallop*! It's **not** a game. I'm a princess.
What's a princess? And *why* do you want to be one?

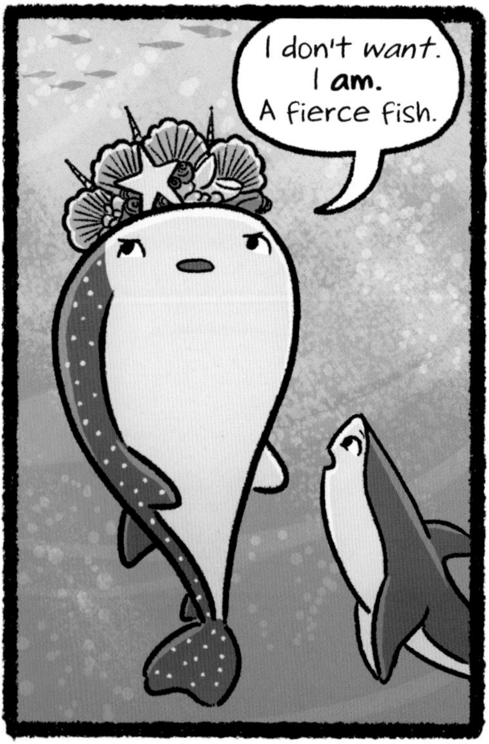
I don't *want*. I **am.** A fierce fish.

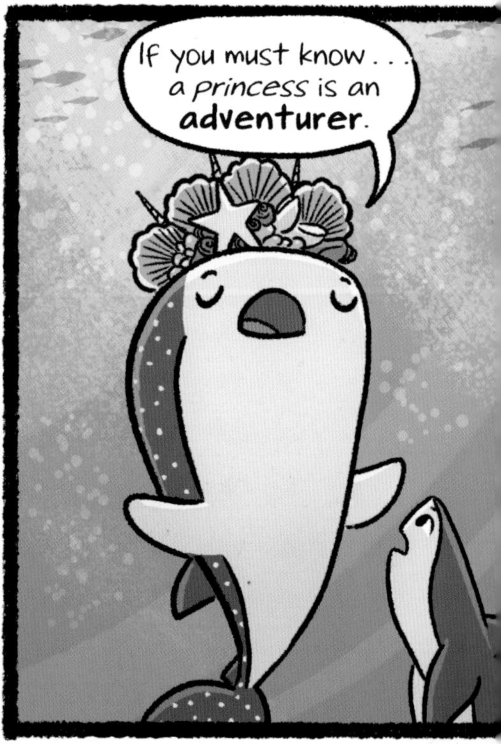
If you must know . . . a *princess* is an **adventurer**.

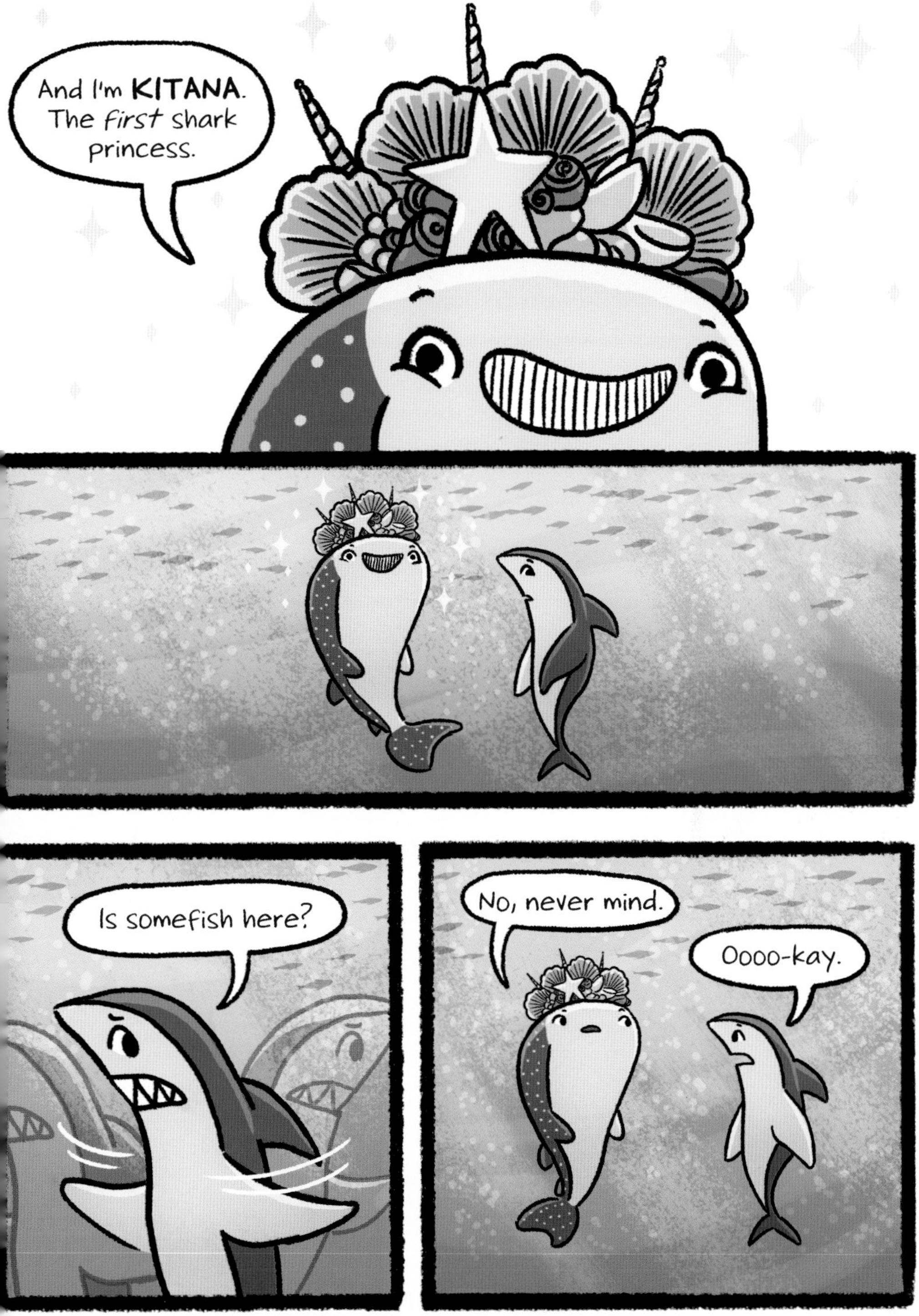
And I'm **KITANA**. The *first* shark princess.
Is somefish here?
No, never mind.
Oooo-kay.

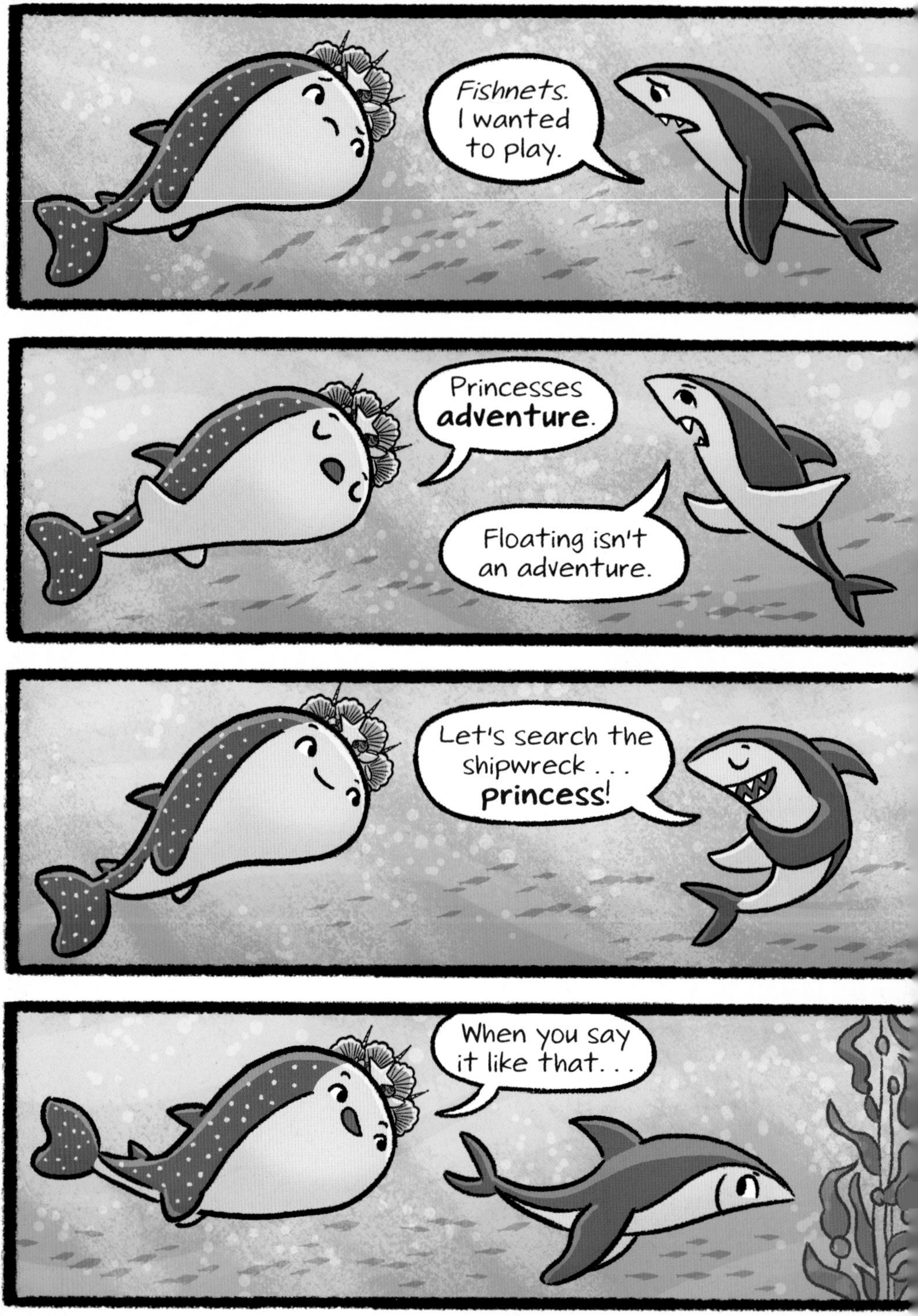
Fishnets. I wanted to play.
Princesses **adventure**.
Floating isn't an adventure.
Let's search the shipwreck . . . **princess**!
When you say it like that. . .

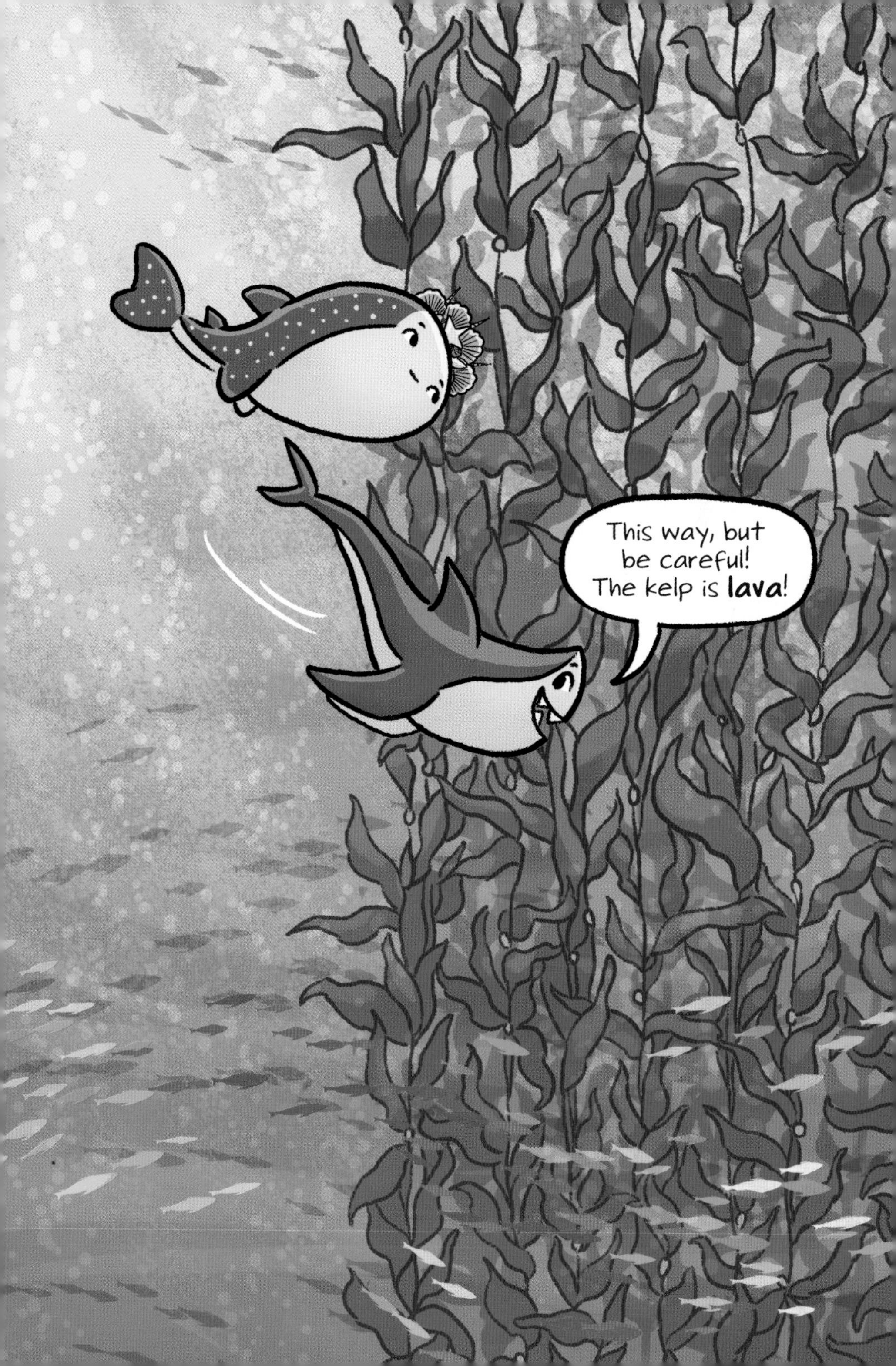
This way, but be careful! The kelp is **lava**!

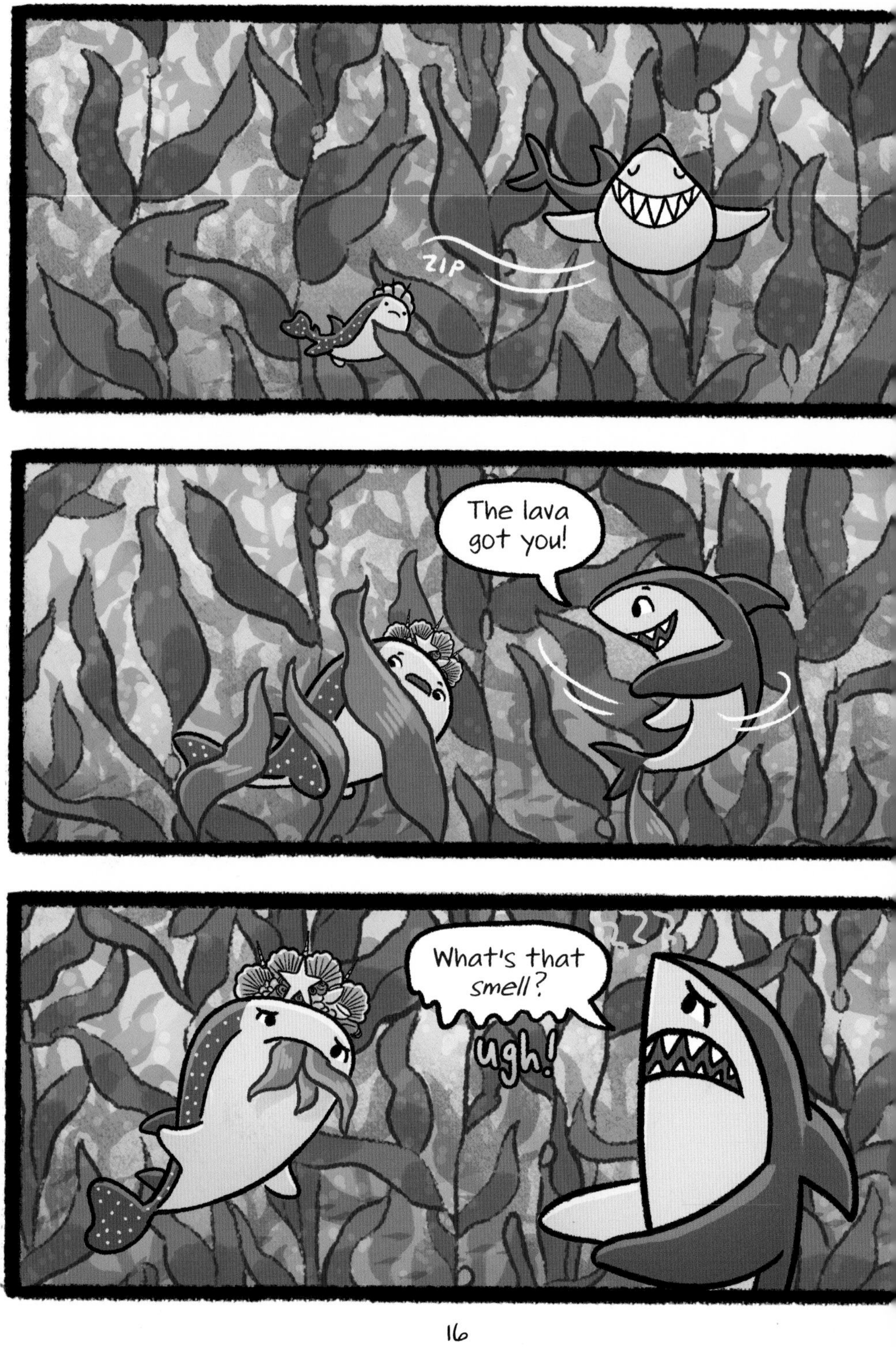
ZIP
The lava got you!
What's that smell?
ugh!

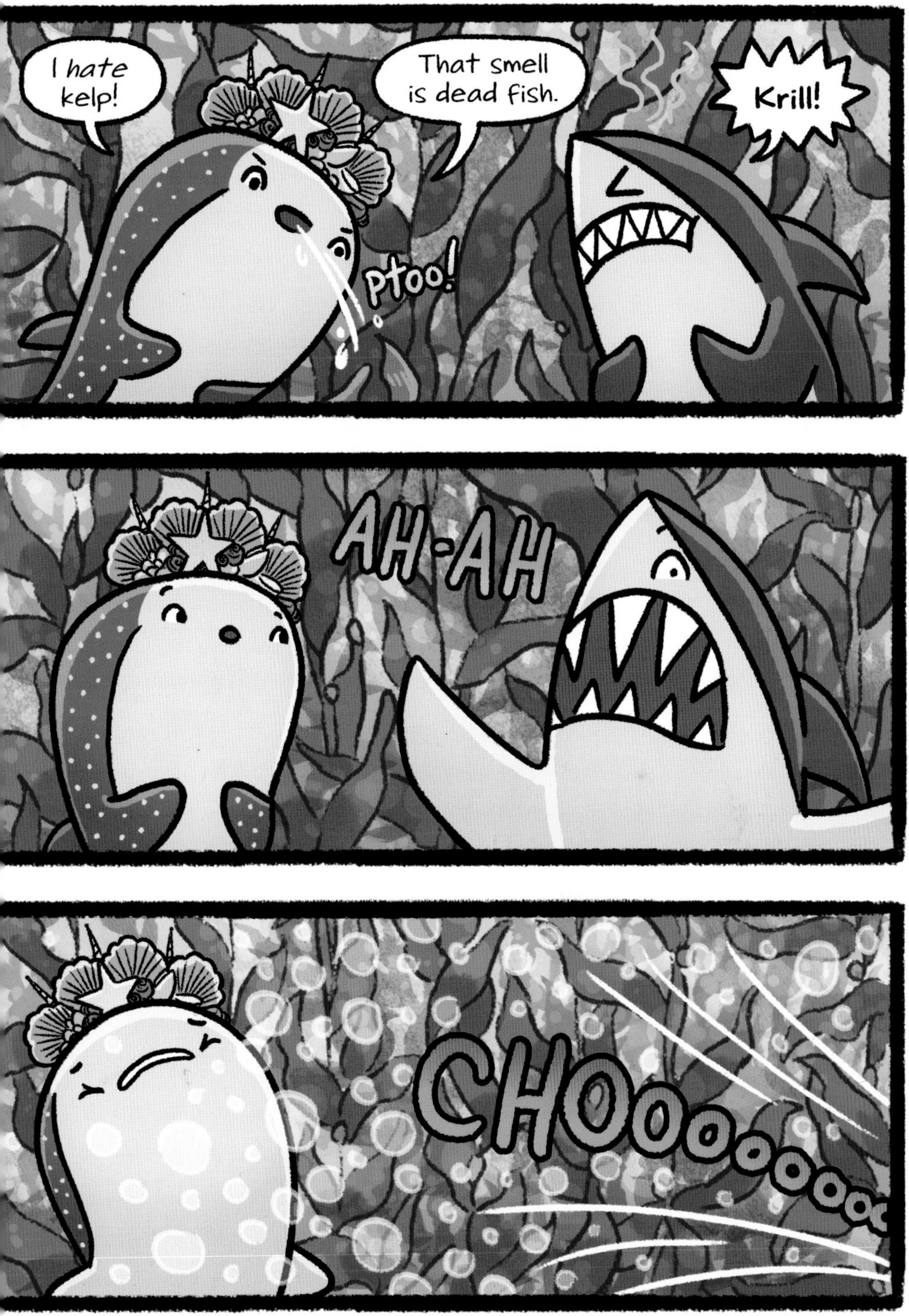
I hate kelp!
Ptoo!
That smell is dead fish.
Krill!
AH-AH
CHOooooooo

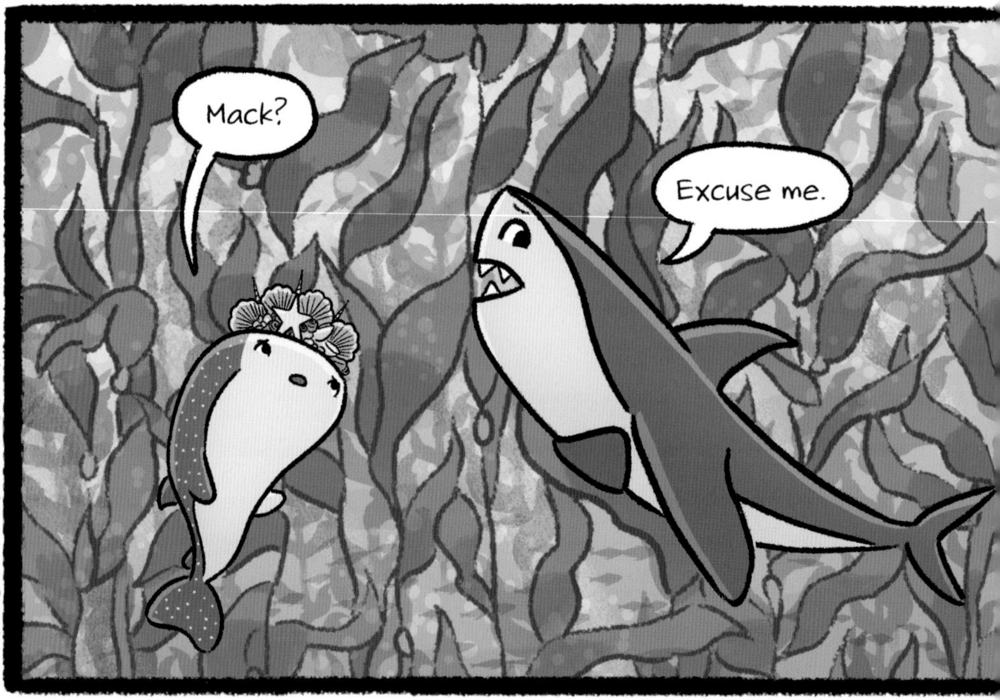
Mack?
Excuse me.

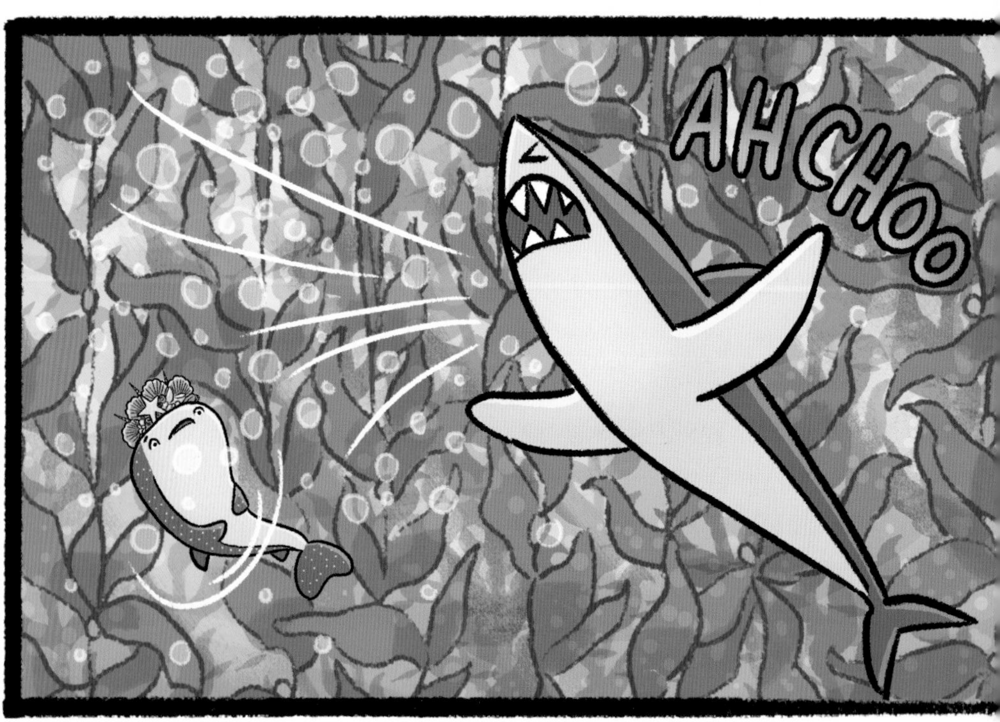
AHCHOO

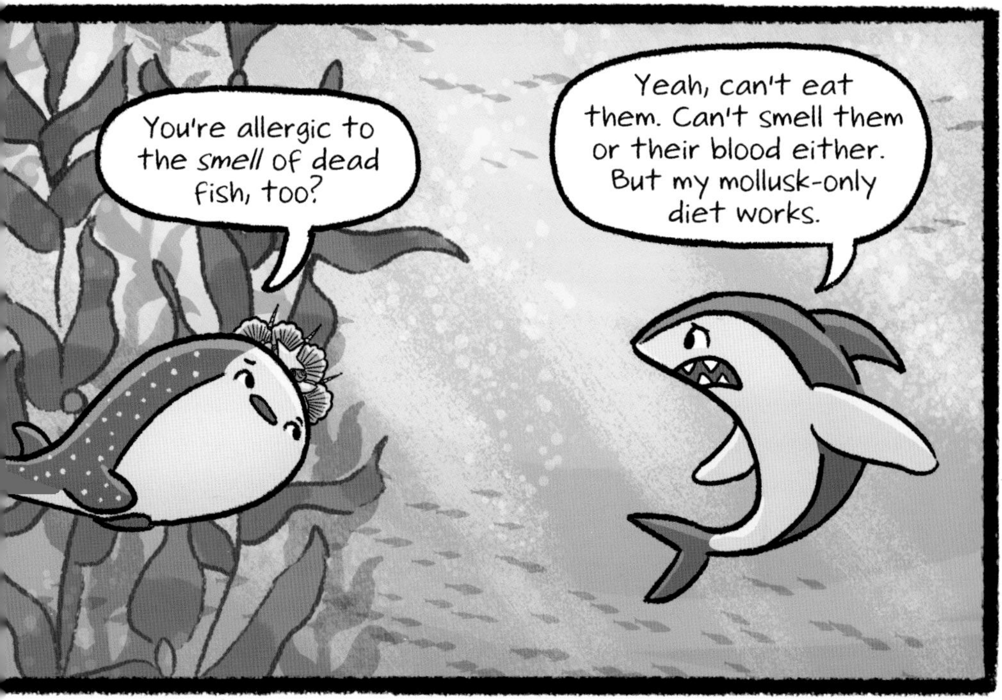
You're allergic to the *smell* of dead fish, too?
Yeah, can't eat them. Can't smell them or their blood either. But my mollusk-only diet works.

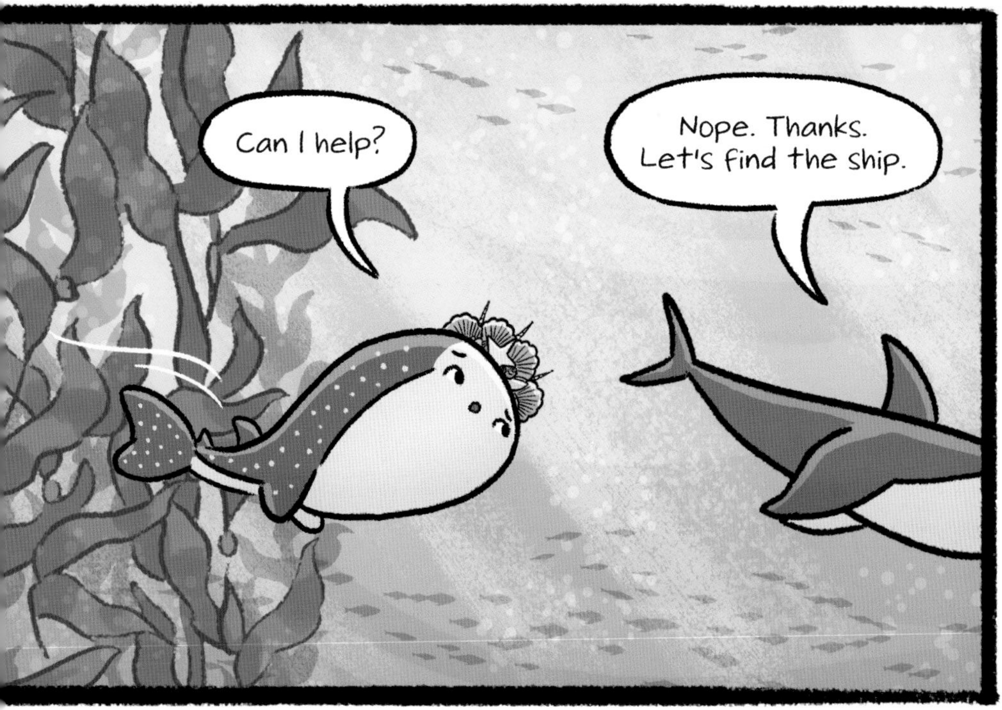
Can I help?
Nope. Thanks. Let's find the ship.

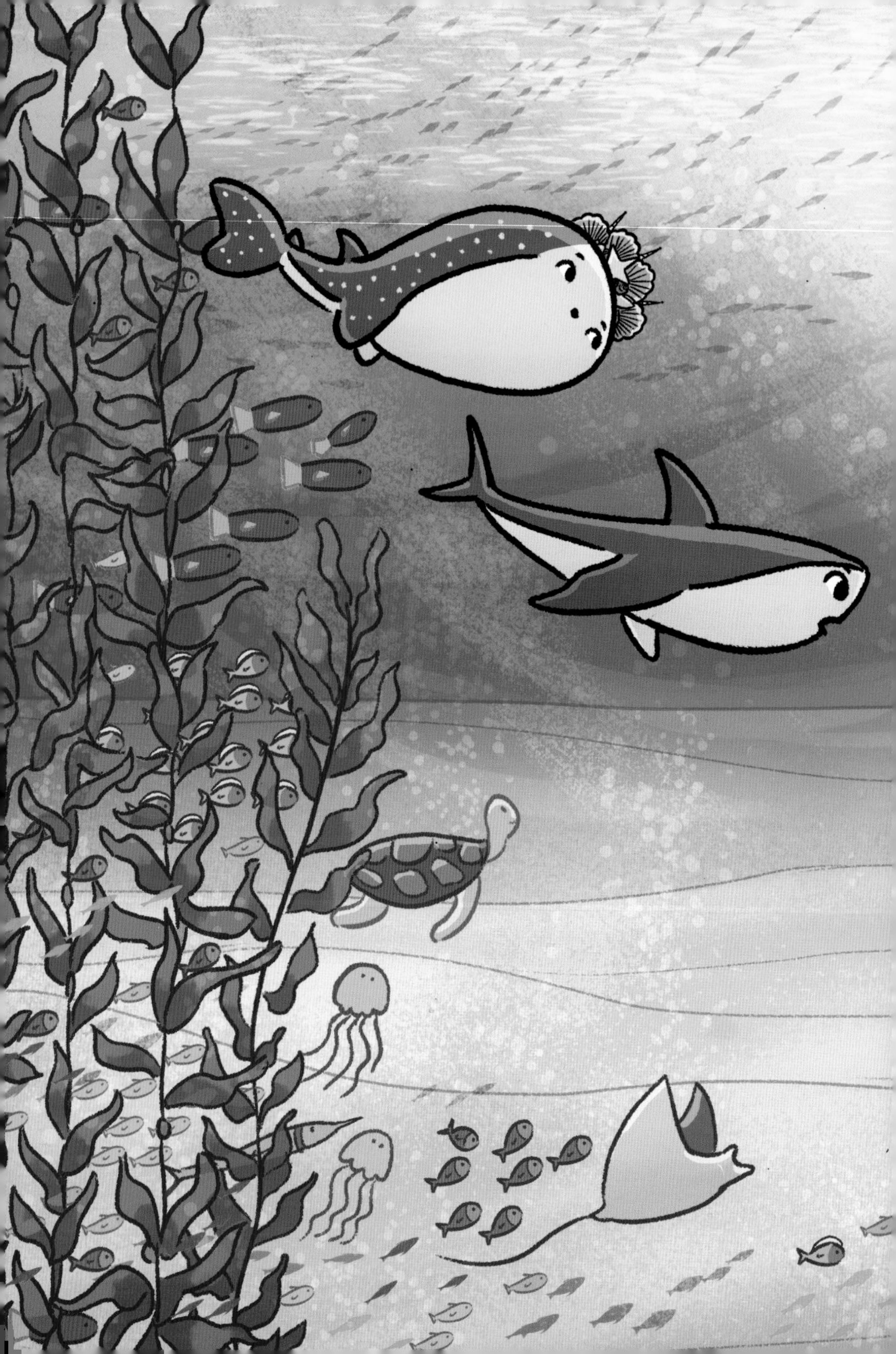

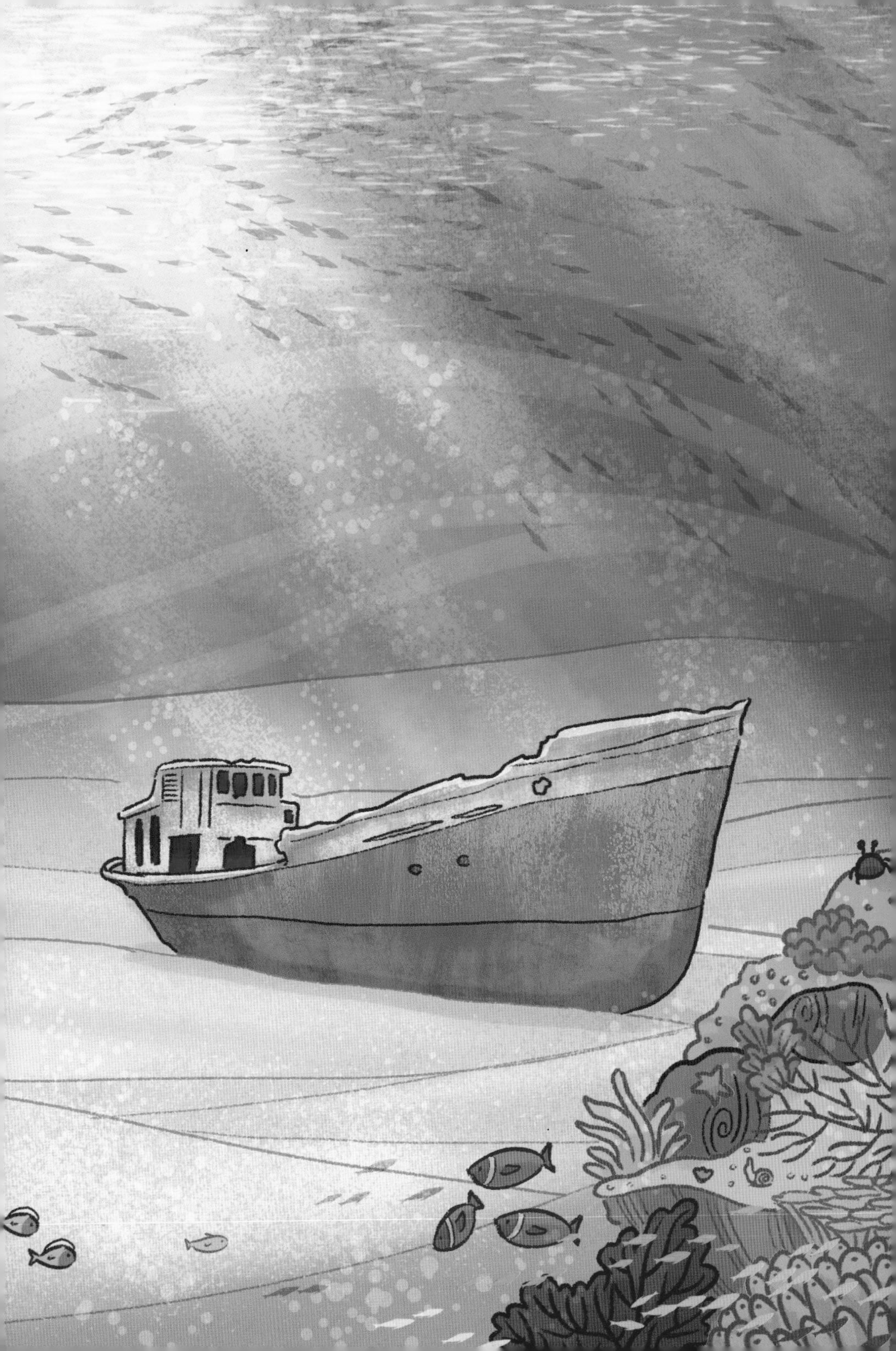

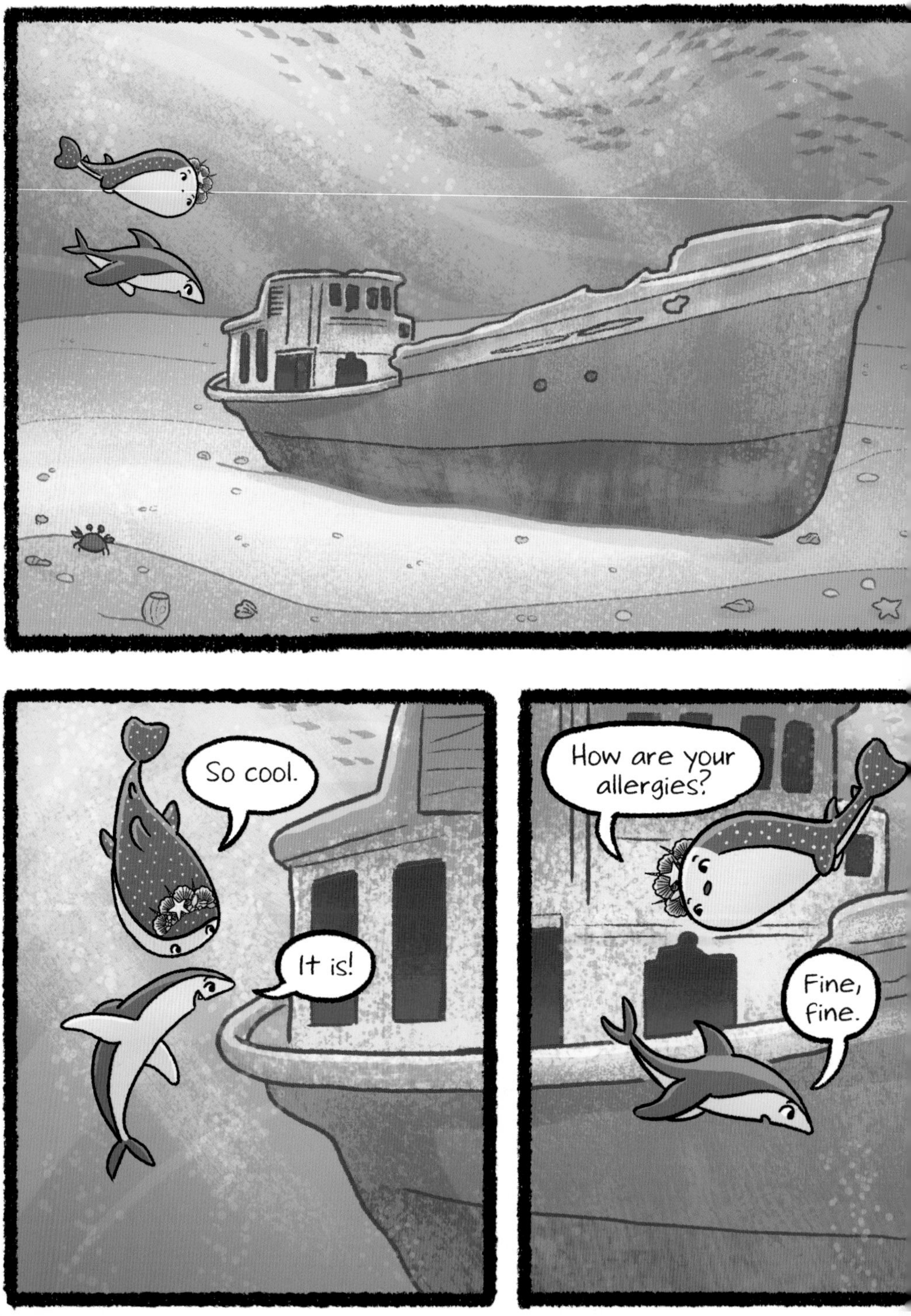
So cool.
It is!
How are your allergies?
Fine, fine.

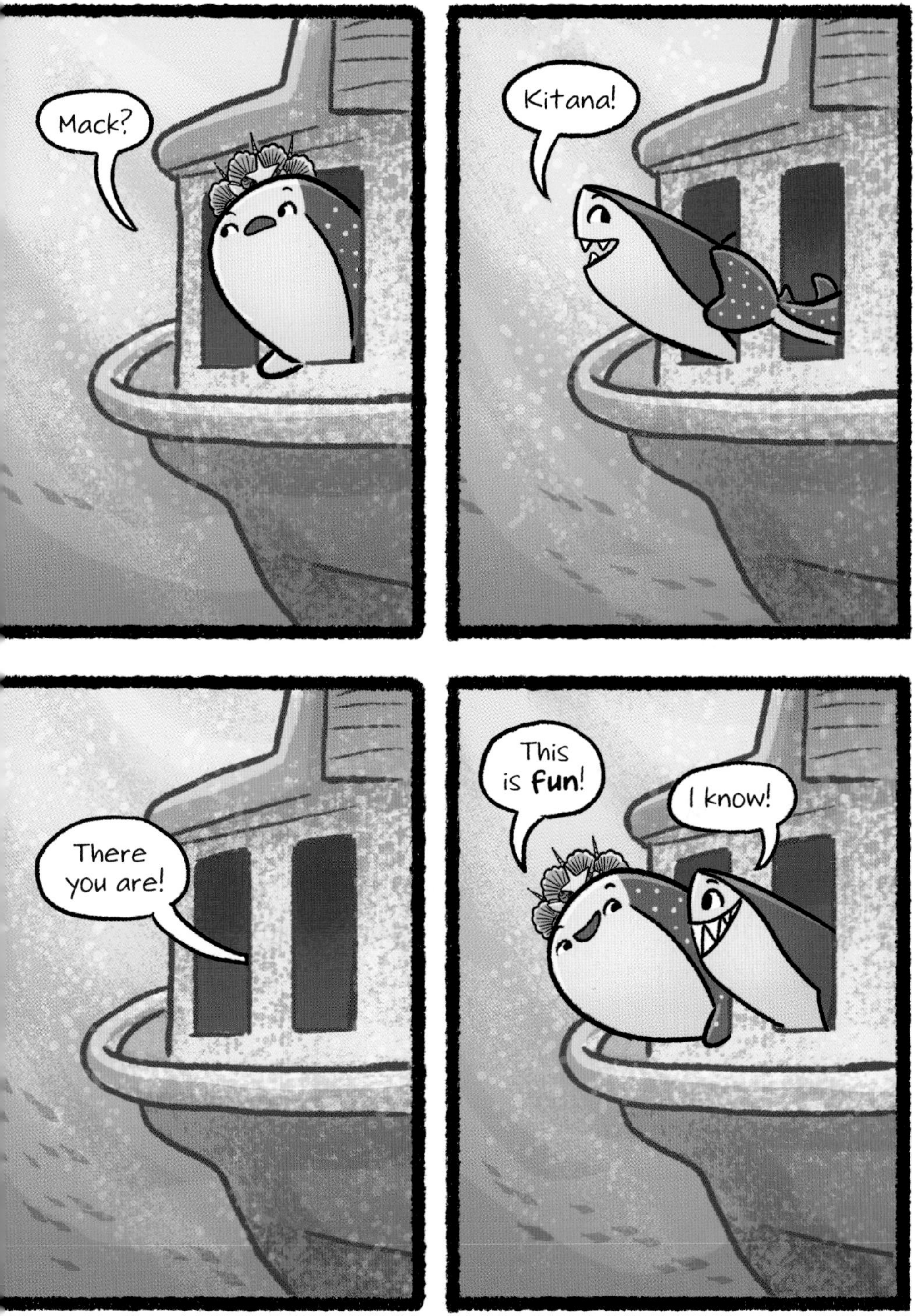
Mack?
Kitana!
There you are!
This is **fun**!
I know!

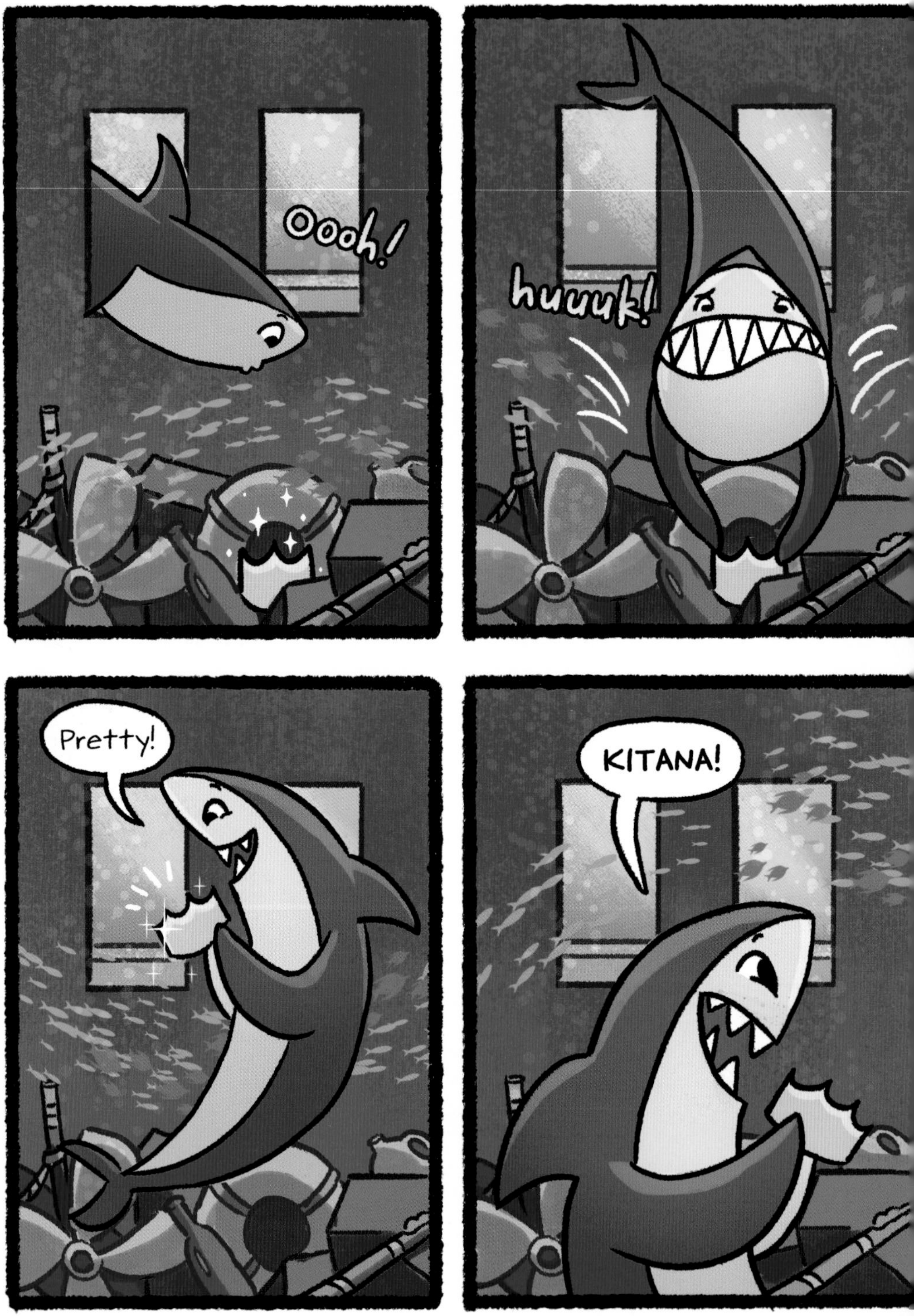
Oooh!
huuuk!
Pretty!
KITANA!

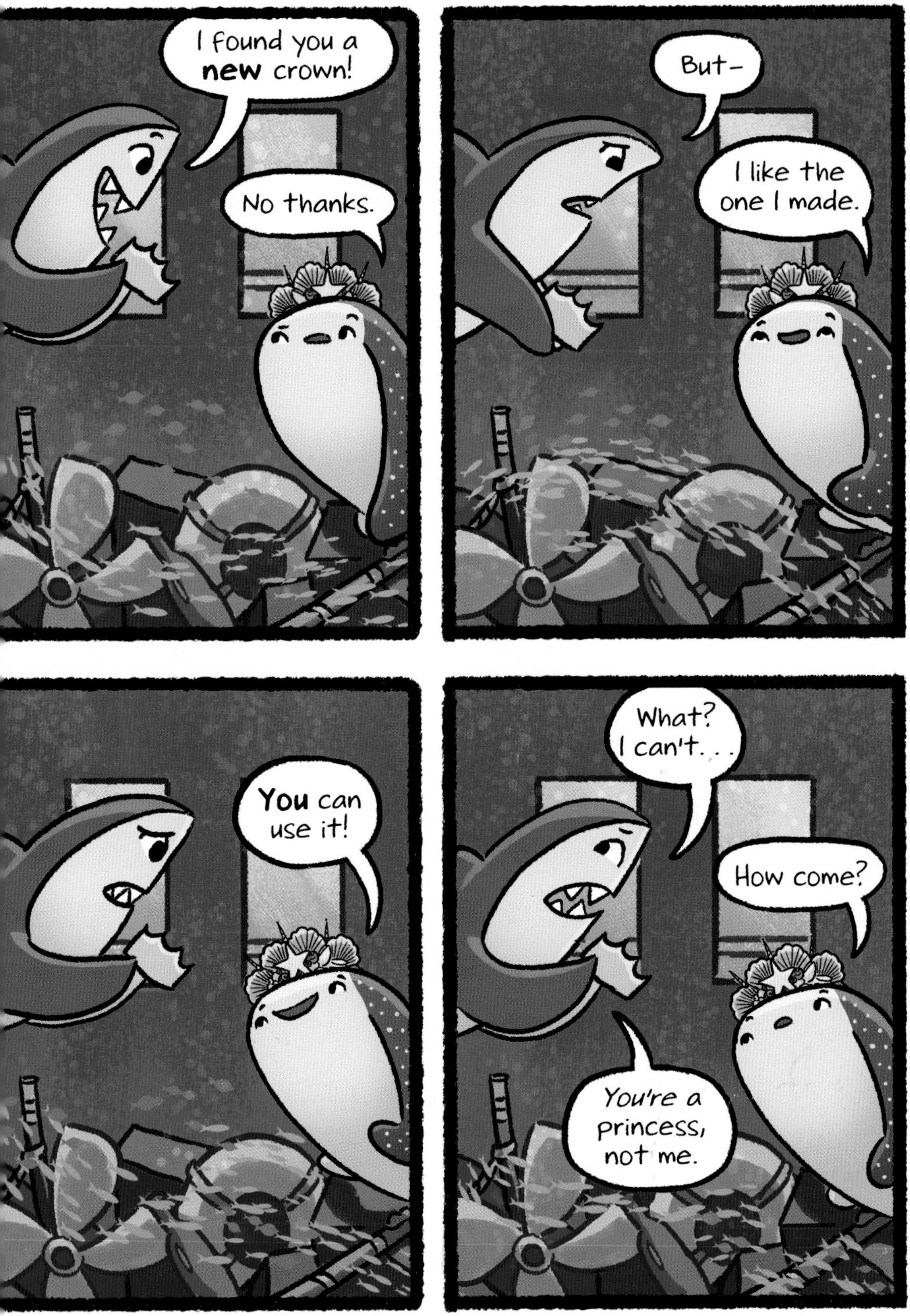
I found you a **new** crown!
No thanks.
But-
I like the one I made.
You can use it!
What? I can't. . .
How come?
You're a princess, not me.

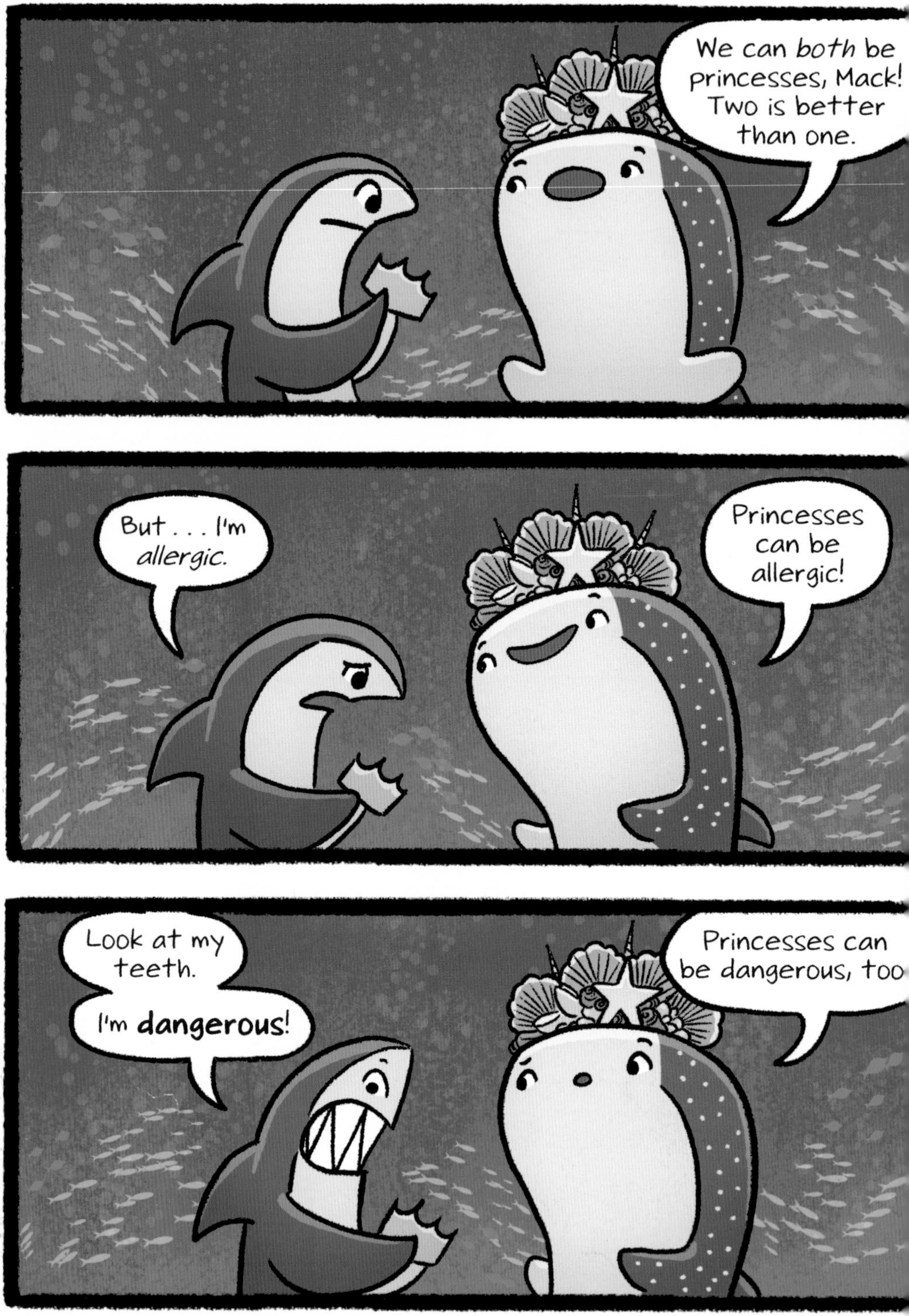
We can *both* be princesses, Mack! Two is better than one.
But . . . I'm *allergic.*
Princesses can be allergic!
Look at my teeth.
I'm **dangerous**!
Princesses can be dangerous, too

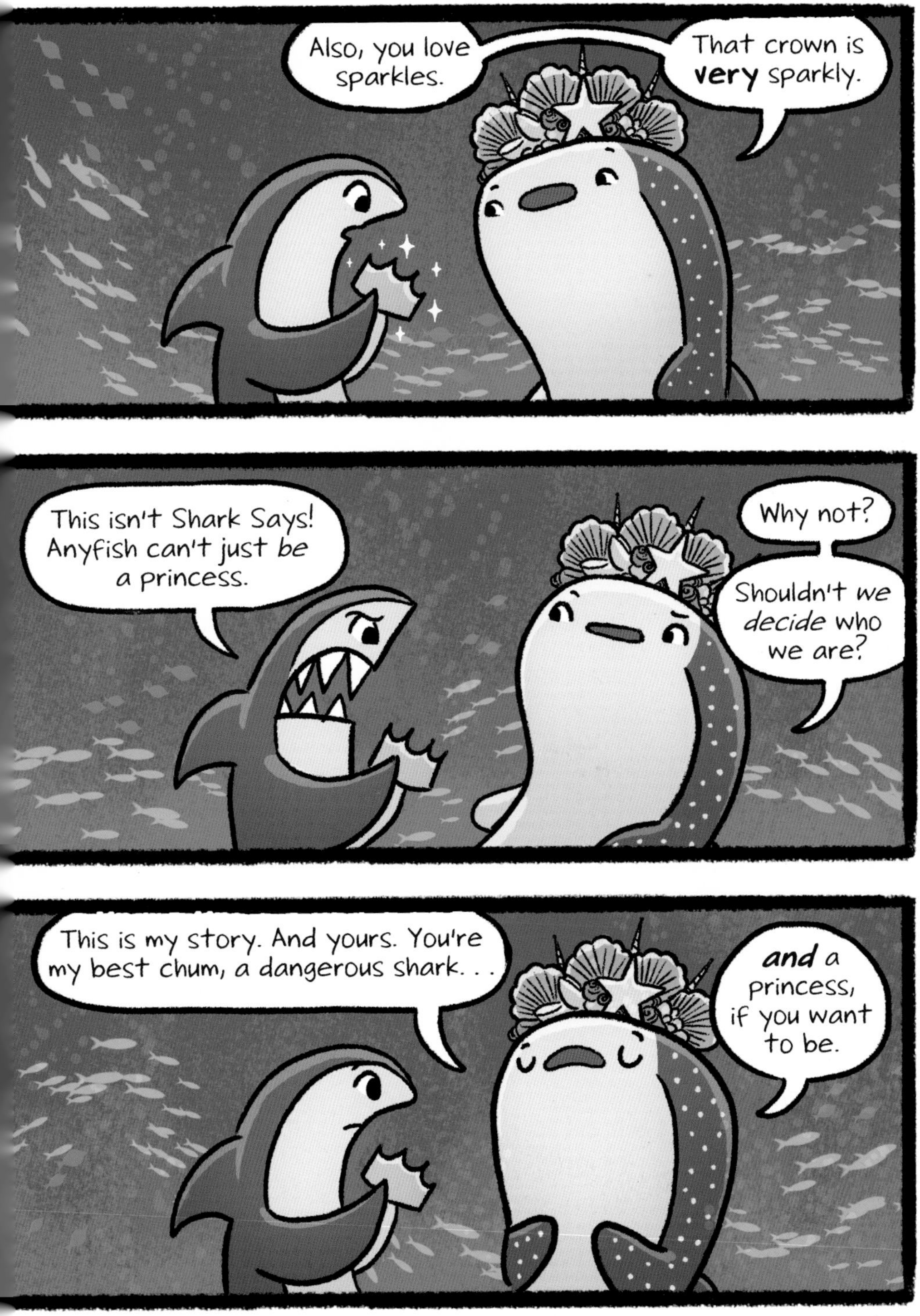
Also, you love sparkles.
That crown is **very** sparkly.
This isn't Shark Says! Anyfish can't just *be* a princess.
Why not?
Shouldn't *we decide* who we are?
This is my story. And yours. You're my best chum, a dangerous shark. . .
and a princess, if you want to be.

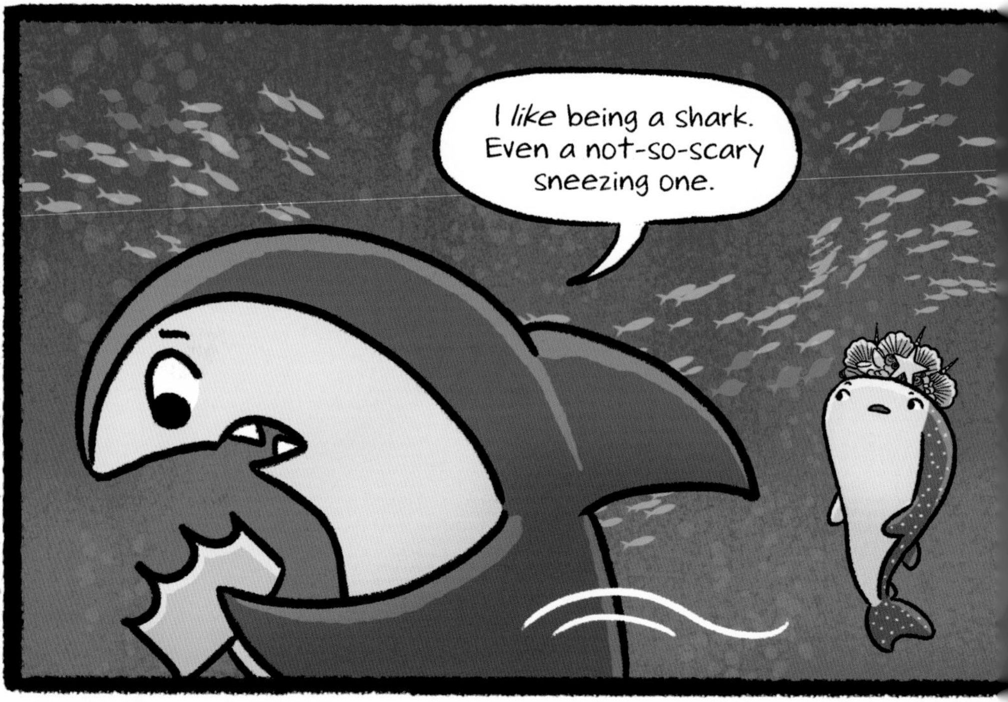
I *like* being a shark. Even a not-so-scary sneezing one.

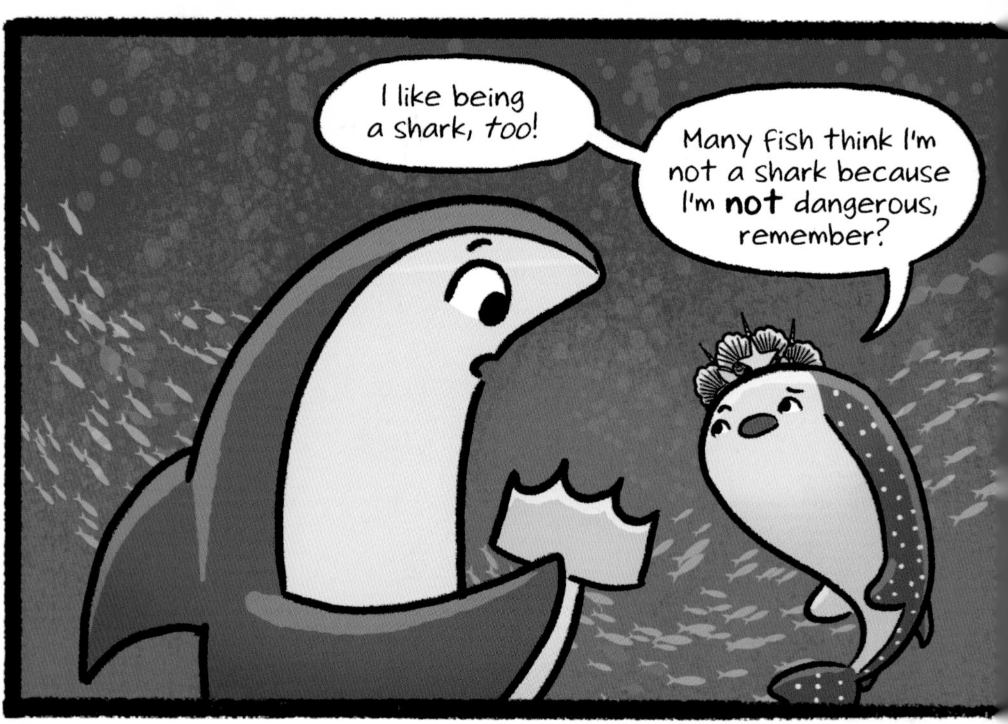
I like being a shark, *too*!
Many fish think I'm not a shark because I'm **not** dangerous, remember?

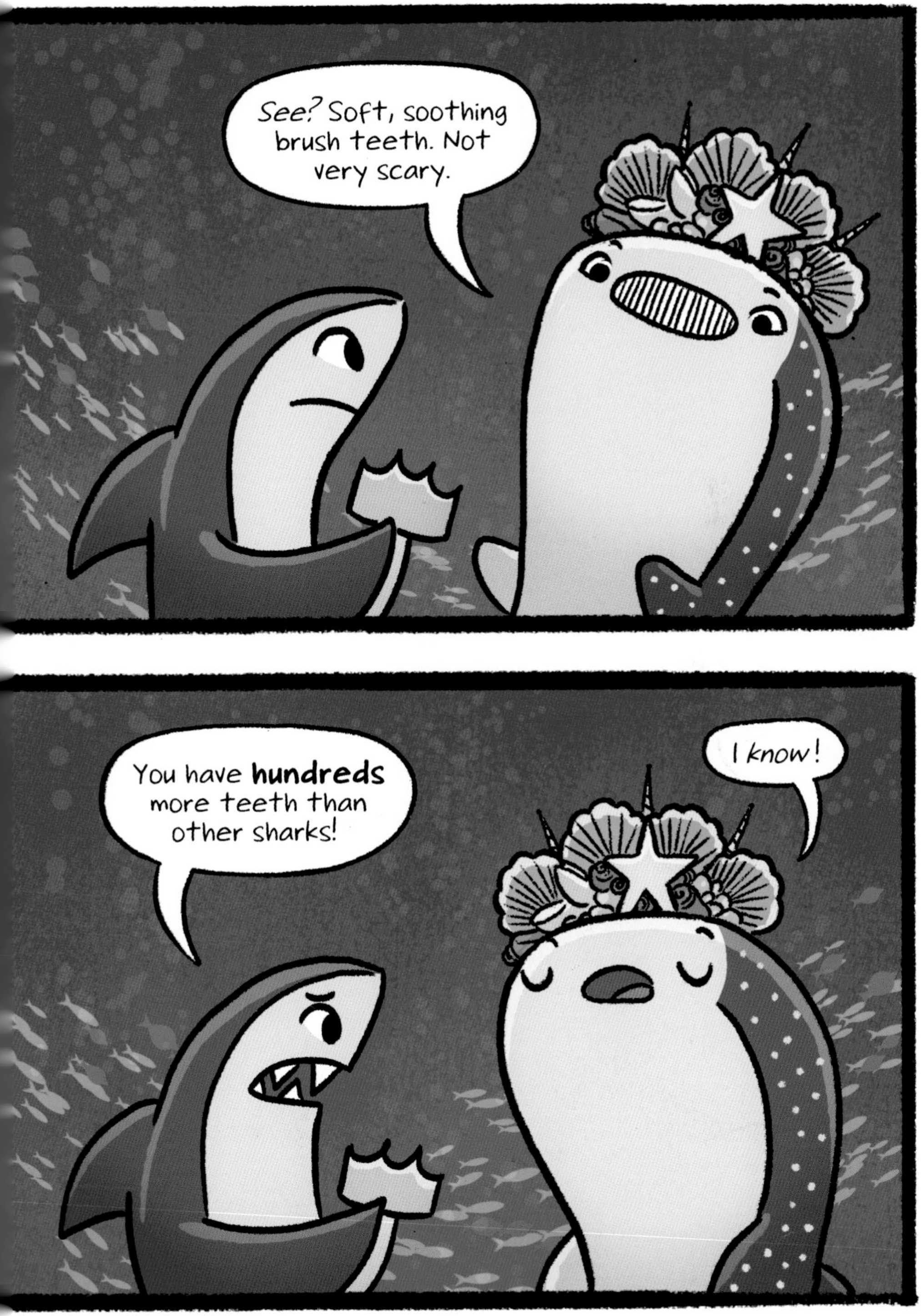

See? Soft, soothing brush teeth. Not very scary.
You have **hundreds** more teeth than other sharks!
I know!

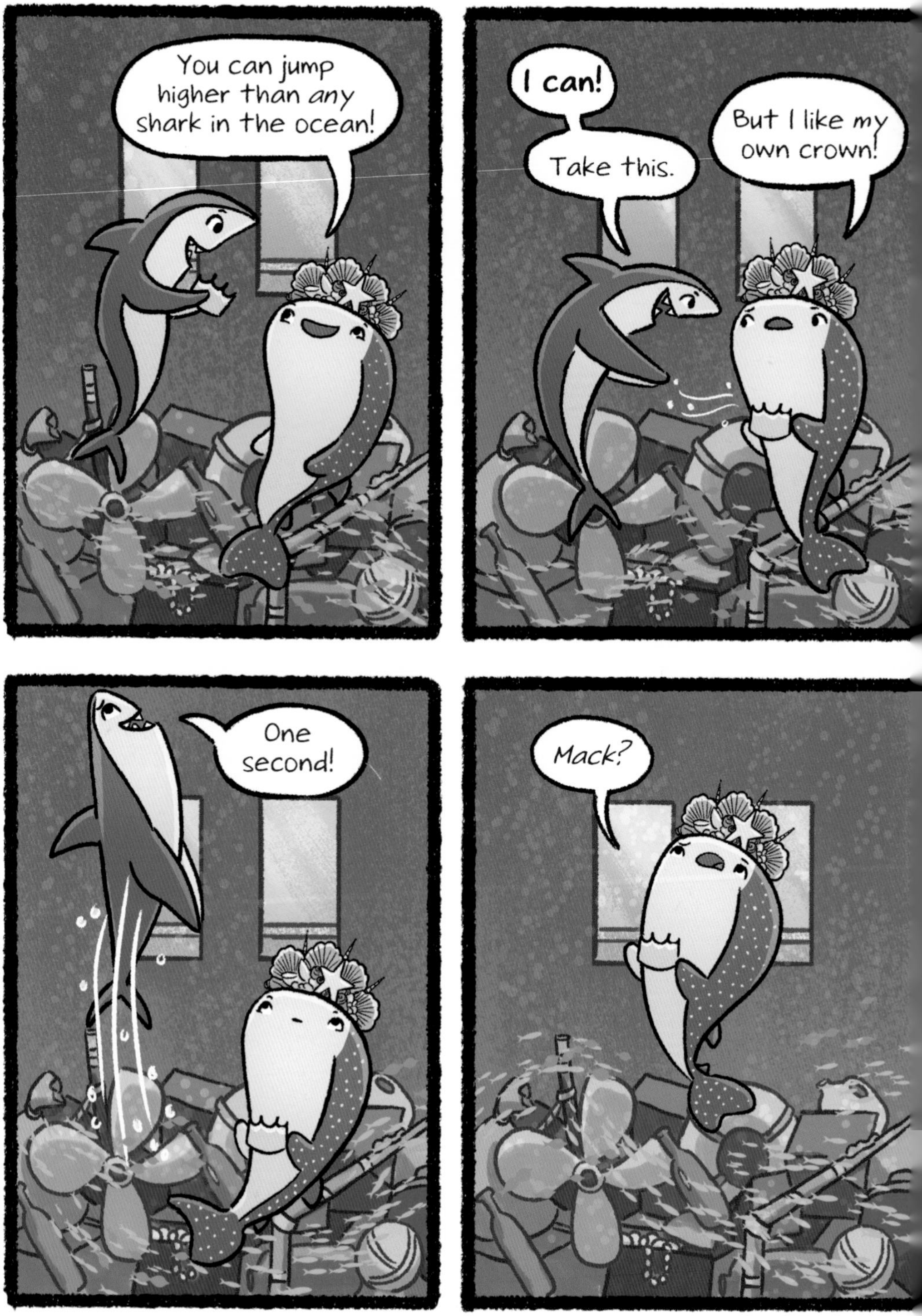
You can jump higher than any shark in the ocean!
I can!
Take this.
But I like my own crown!
One second!
Mack?

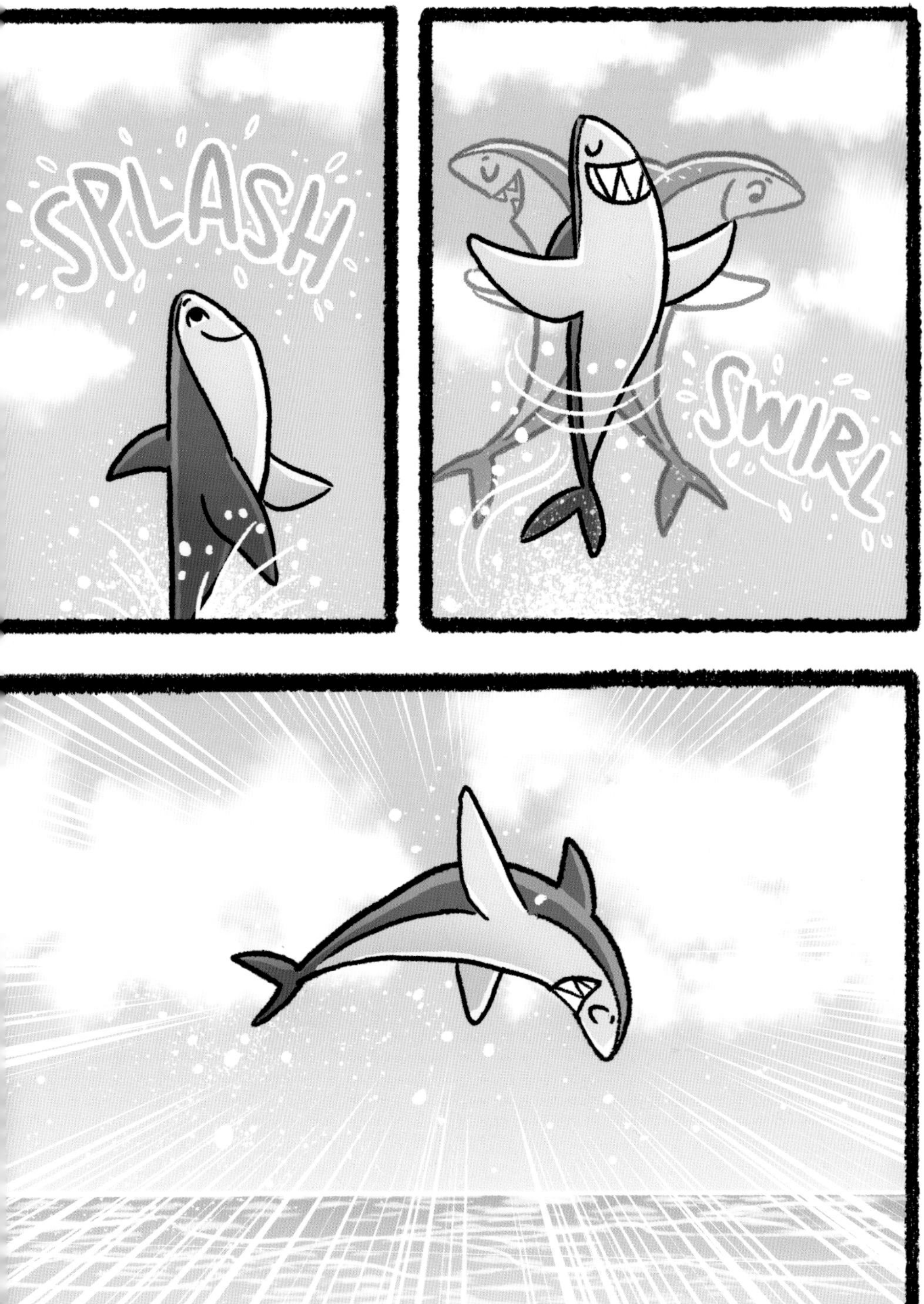
SPLASH
SWIRL

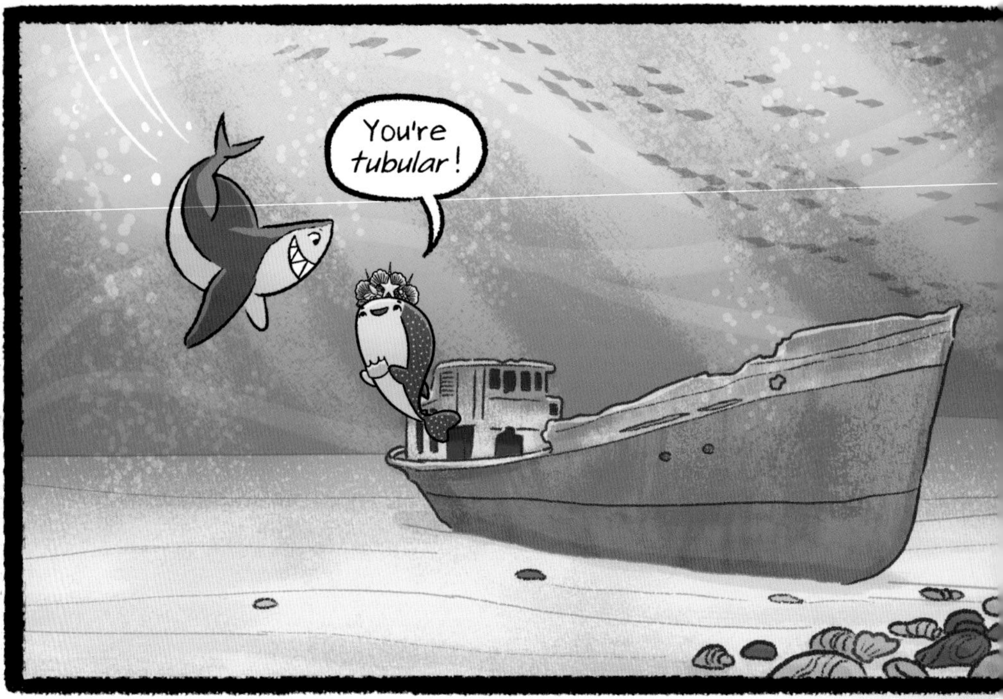
You're tubular!

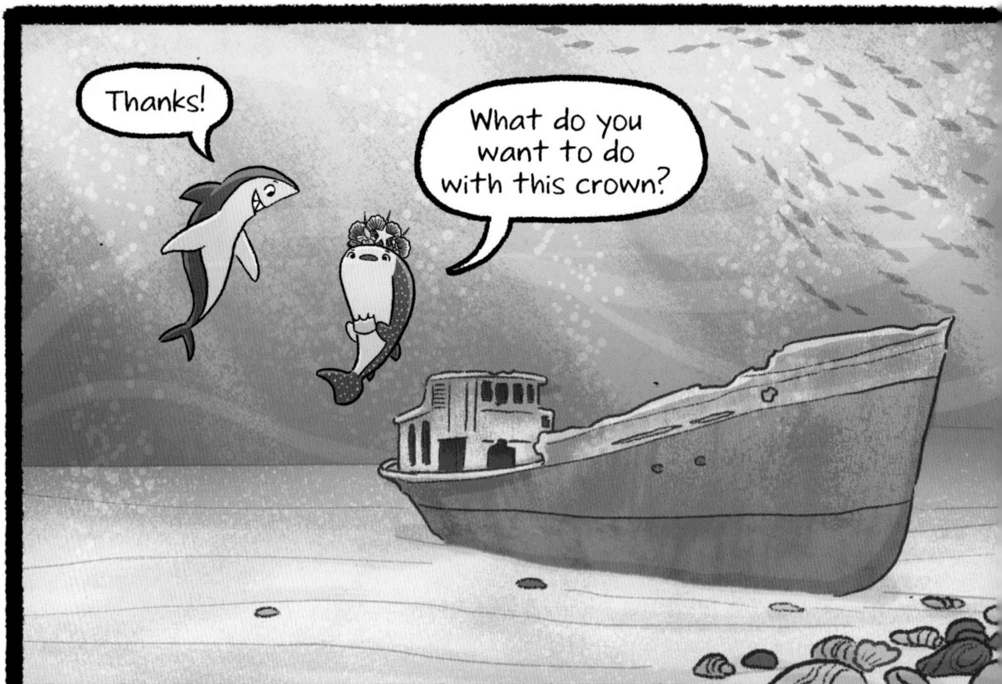
Thanks!
What do you want to do with this crown?

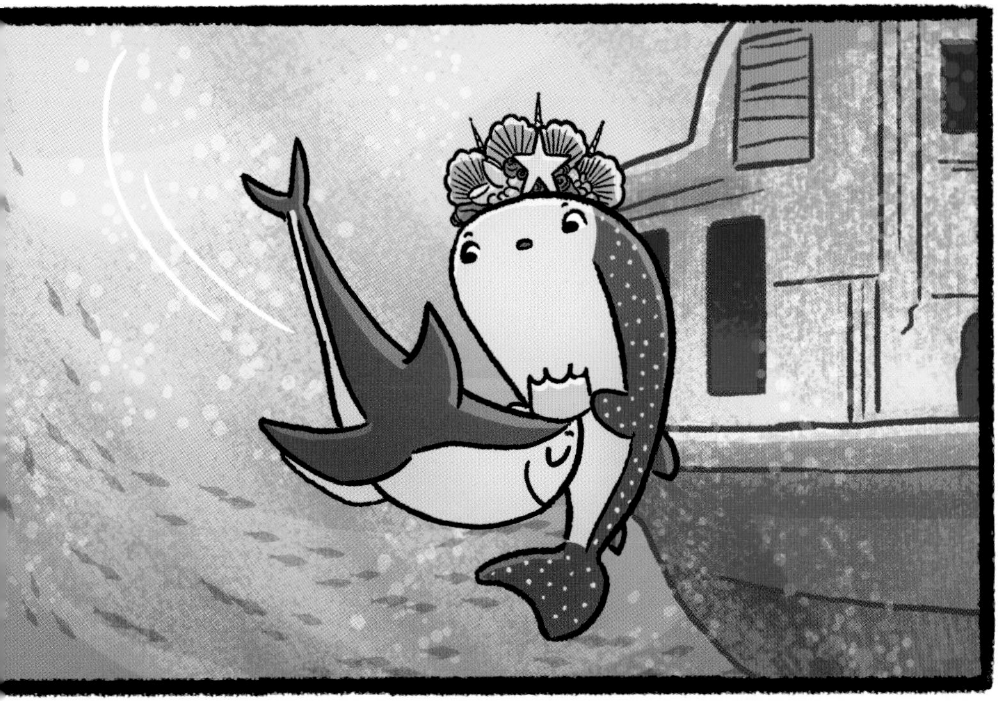

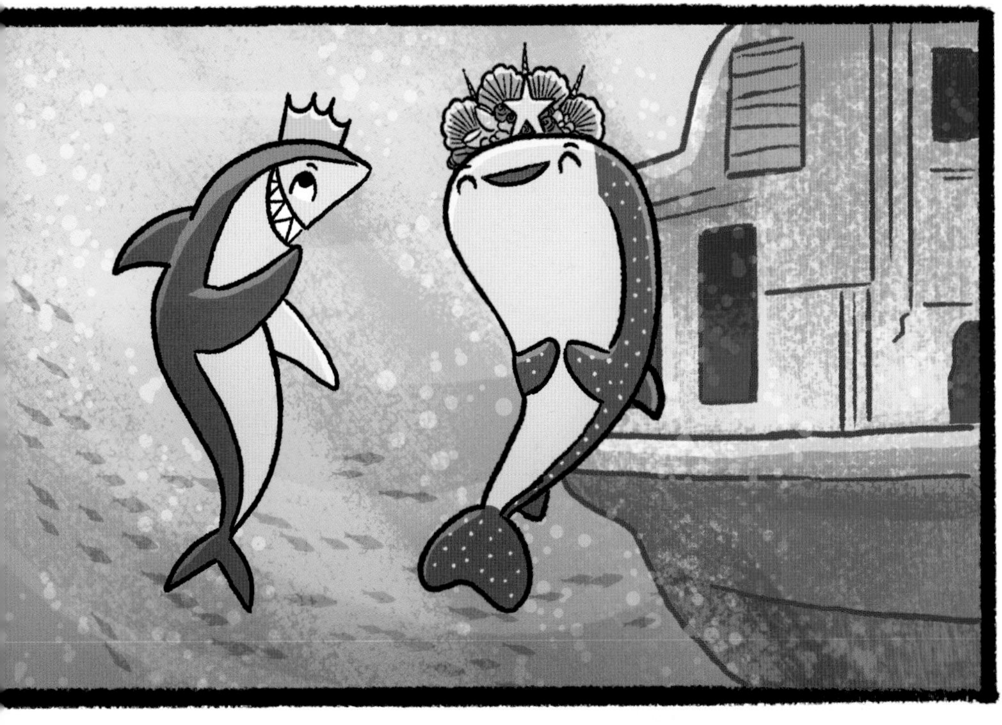

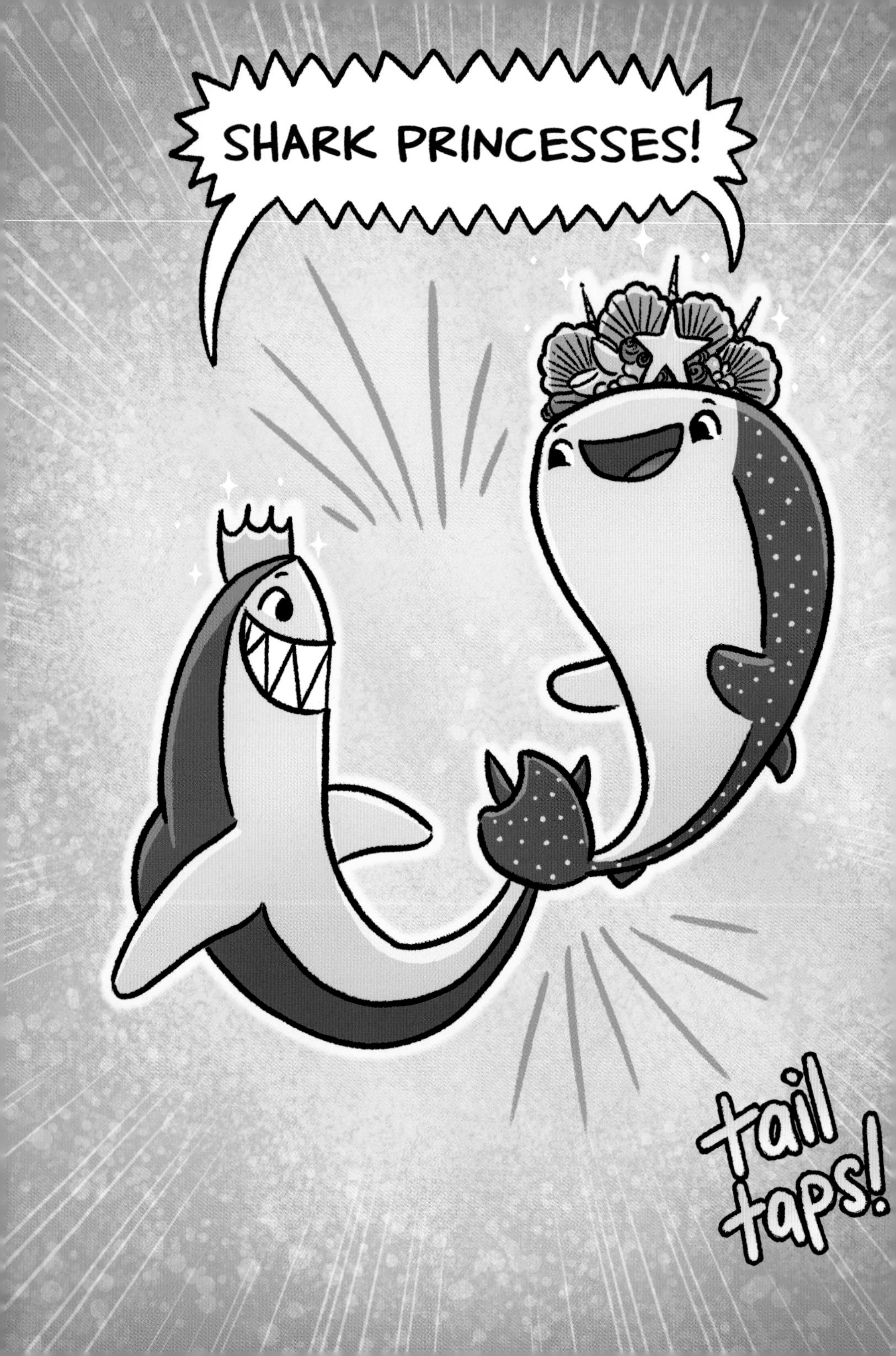
SHARK PRINCESSES!
tail taps!

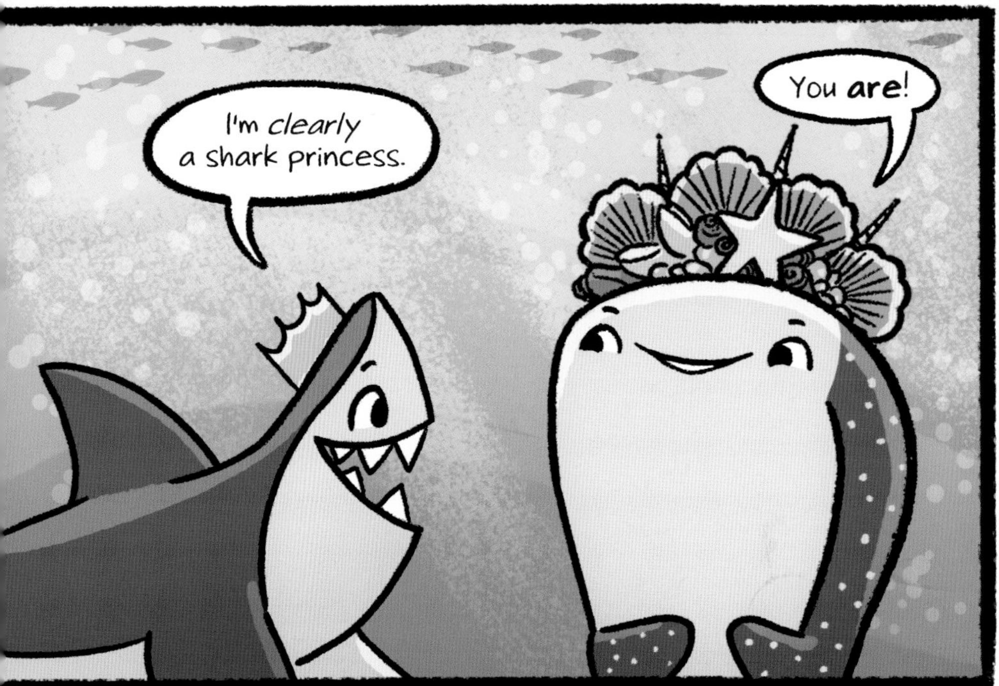
I'm *clearly* a shark princess.
You **are**!

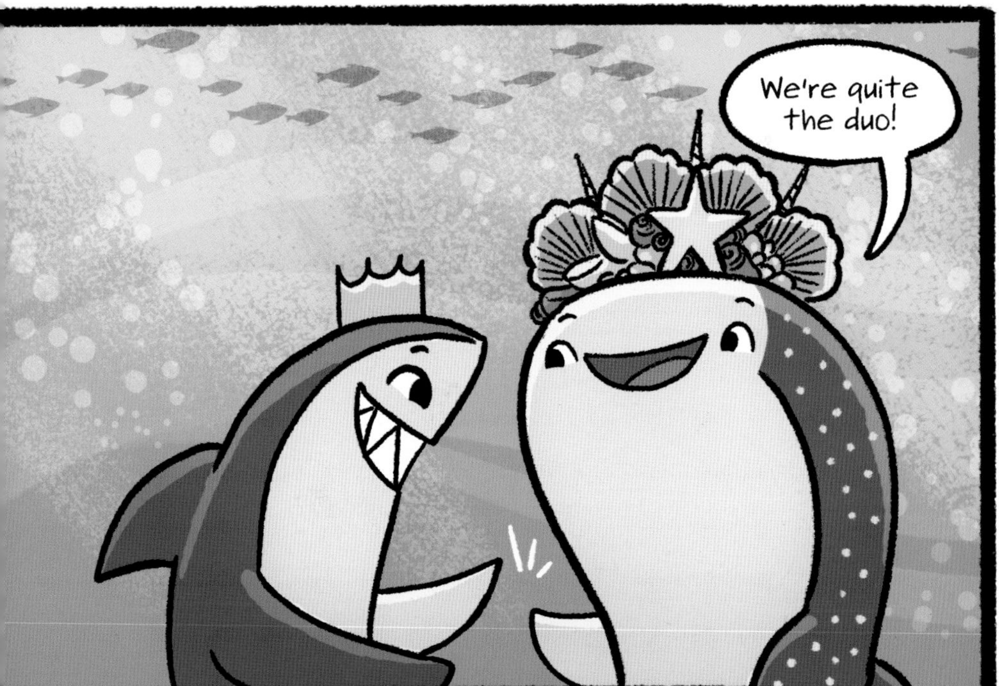
We're quite the duo!

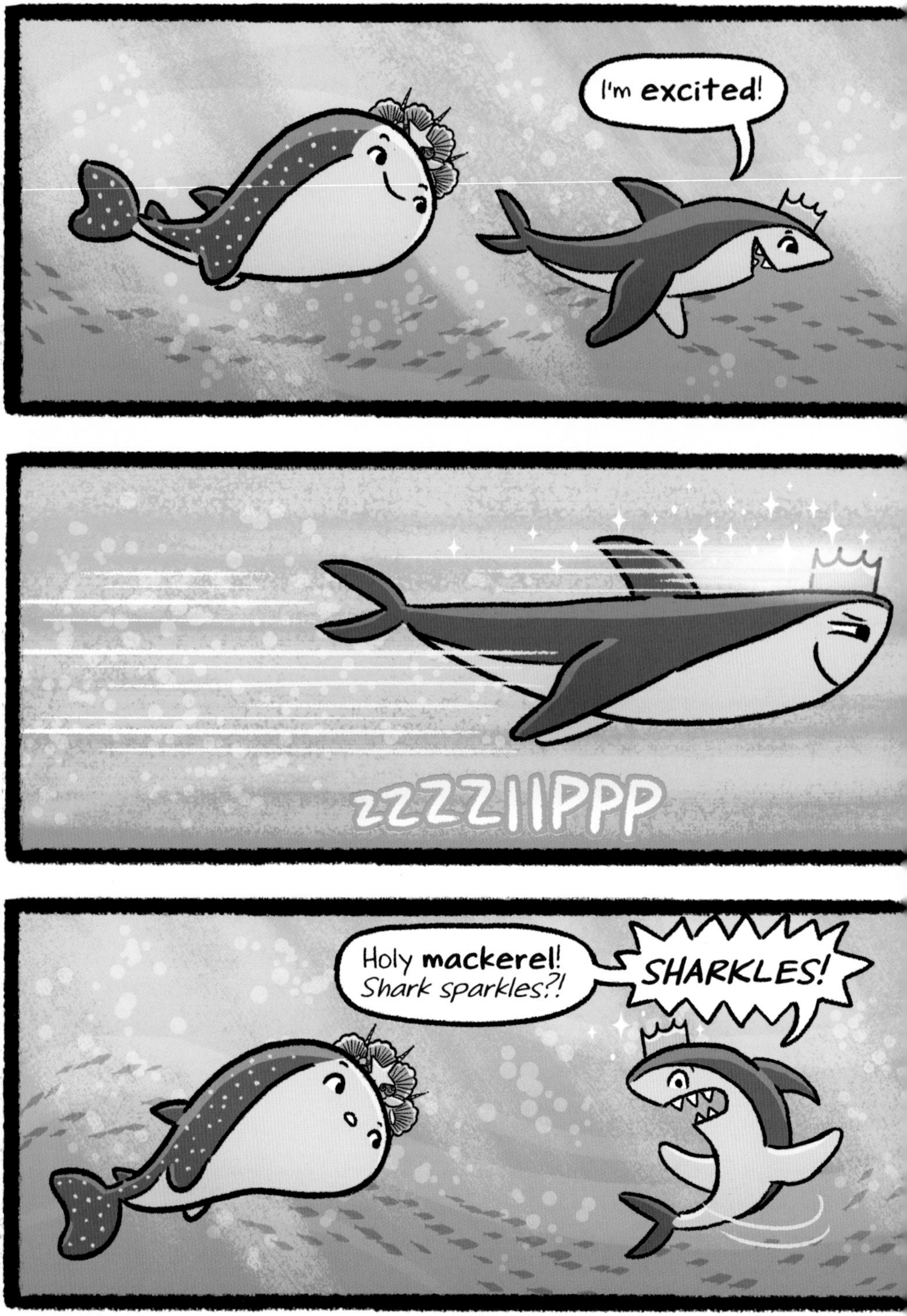
I'm **excited**!
ZZZZIIPPP
Holy **mackerel**! *Shark sparkles?!*
SHARKLES!

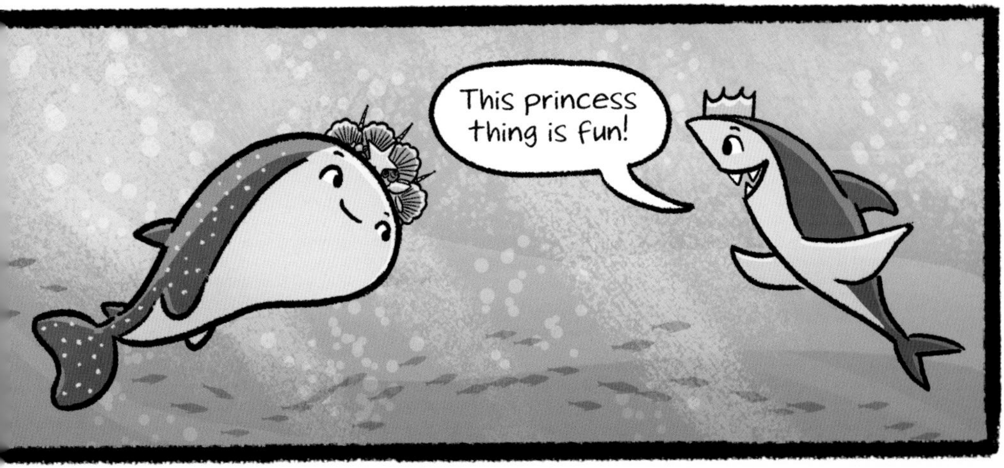
This princess thing is fun!

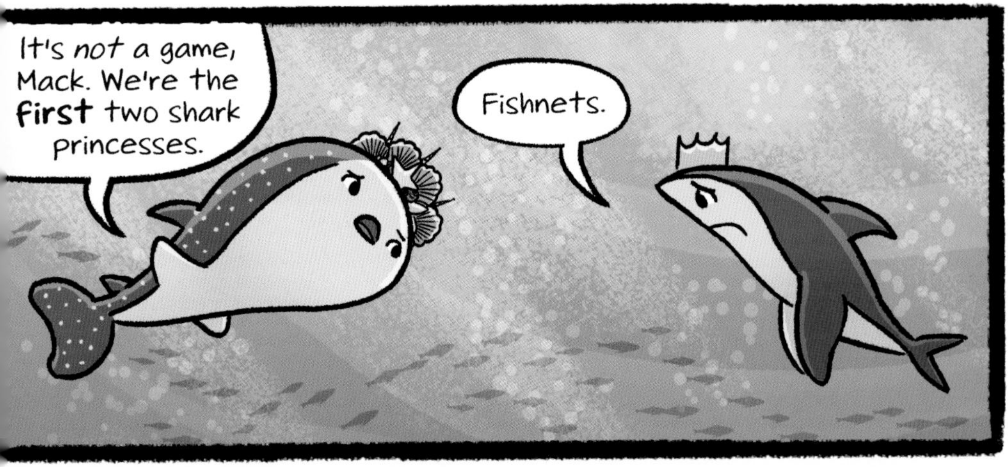
It's *not* a game, Mack. We're the **first** two shark princesses.
Fishnets.

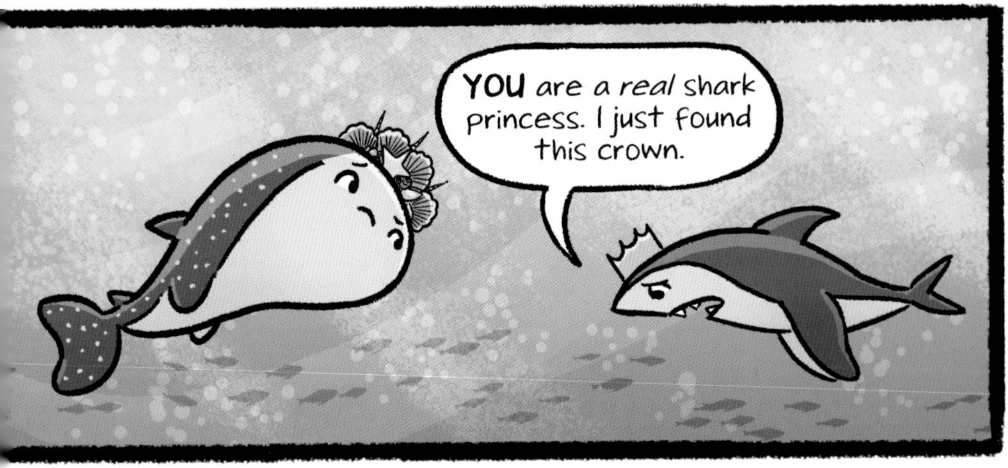
YOU are a *real* shark princess. I just found this crown.

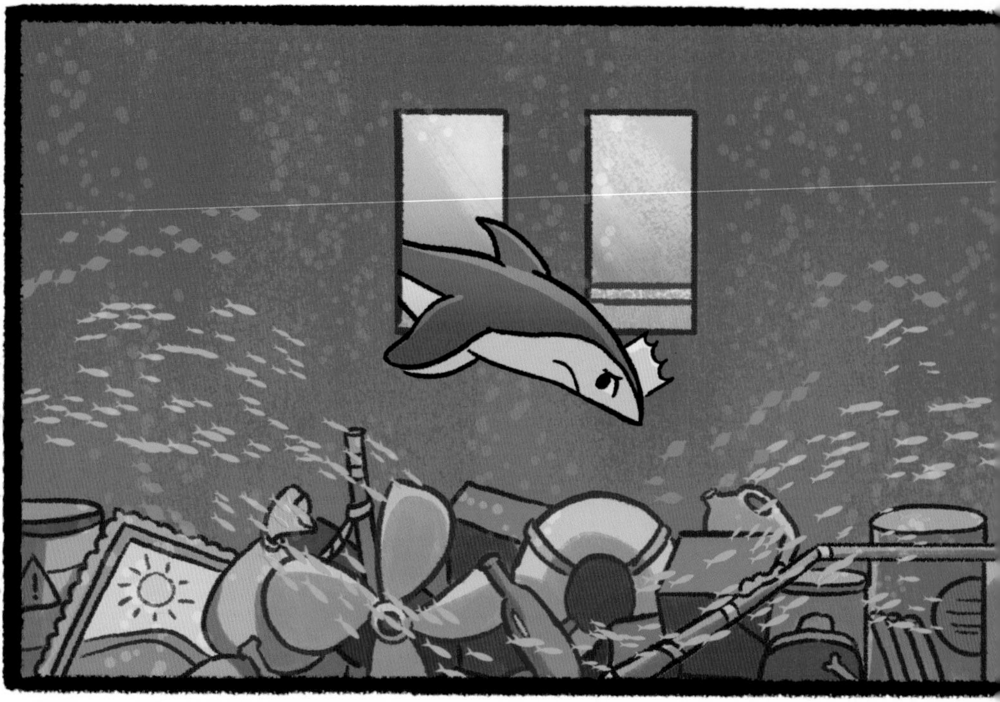

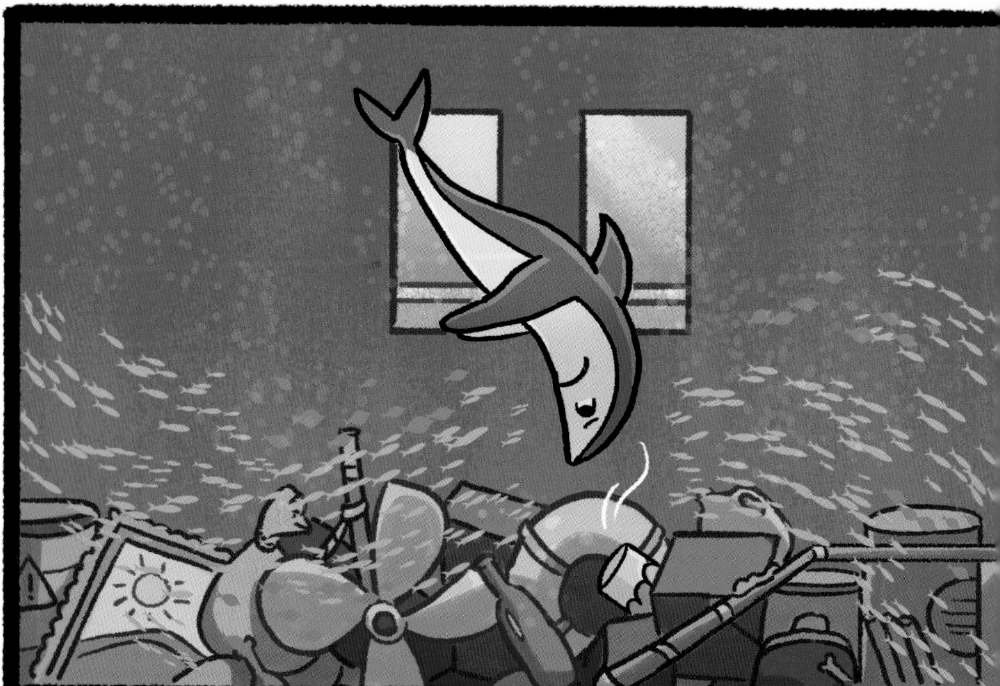

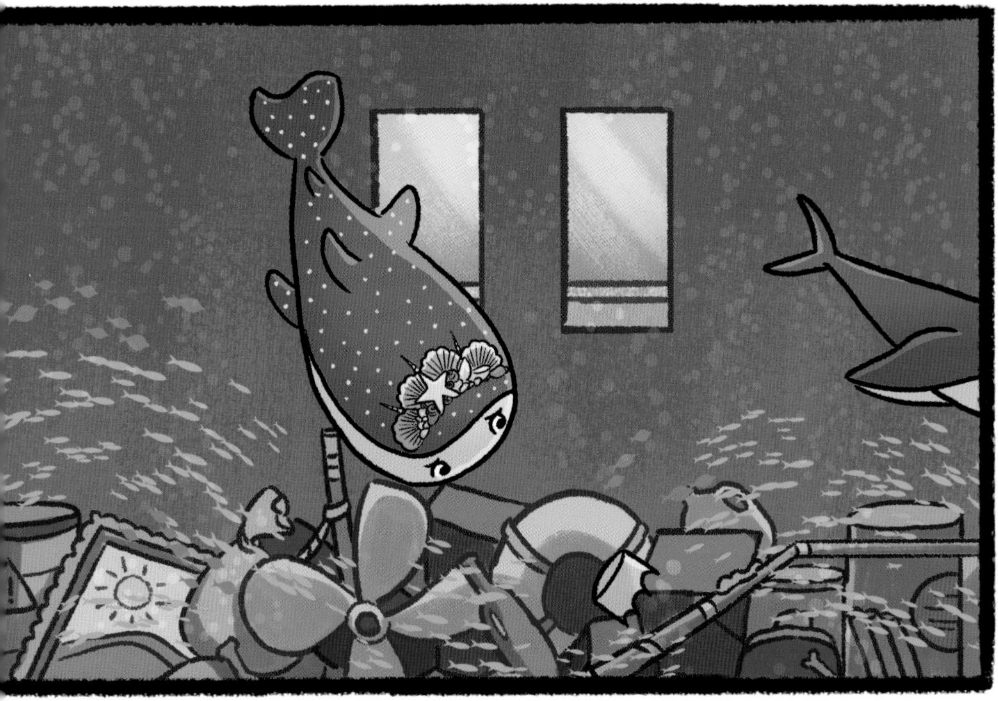

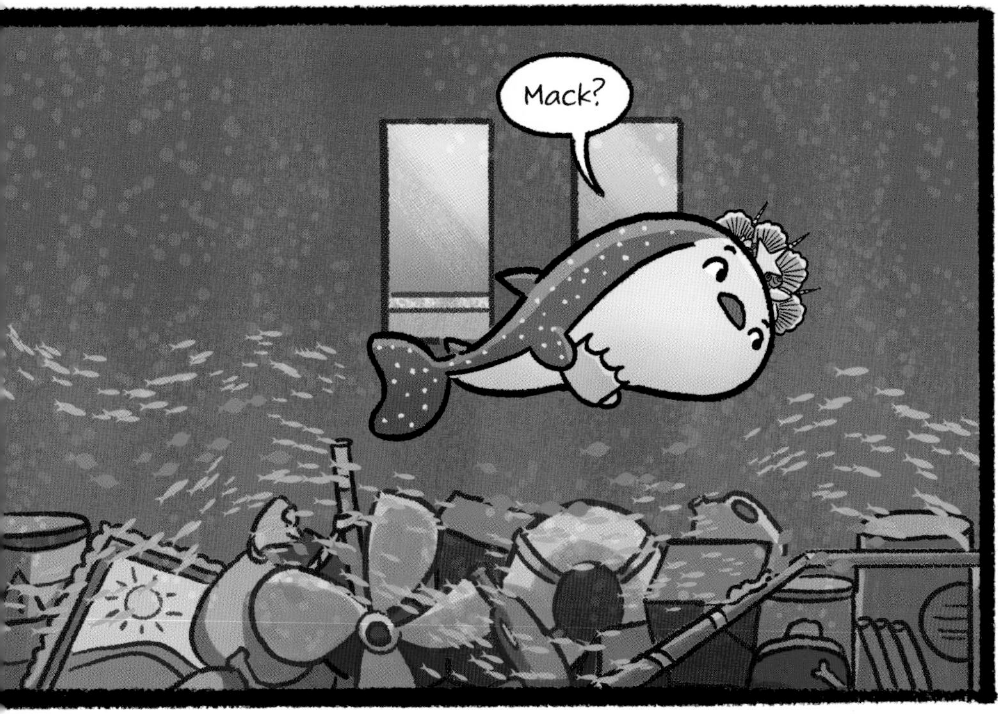
Mack?

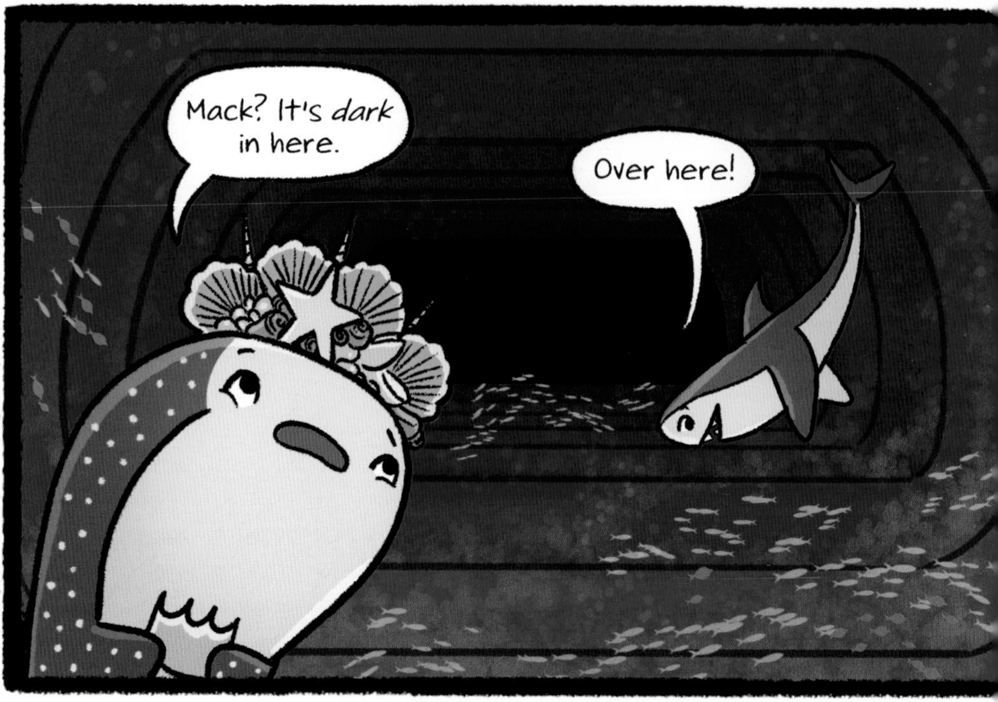
Mack? It's *dark* in here.
Over here!

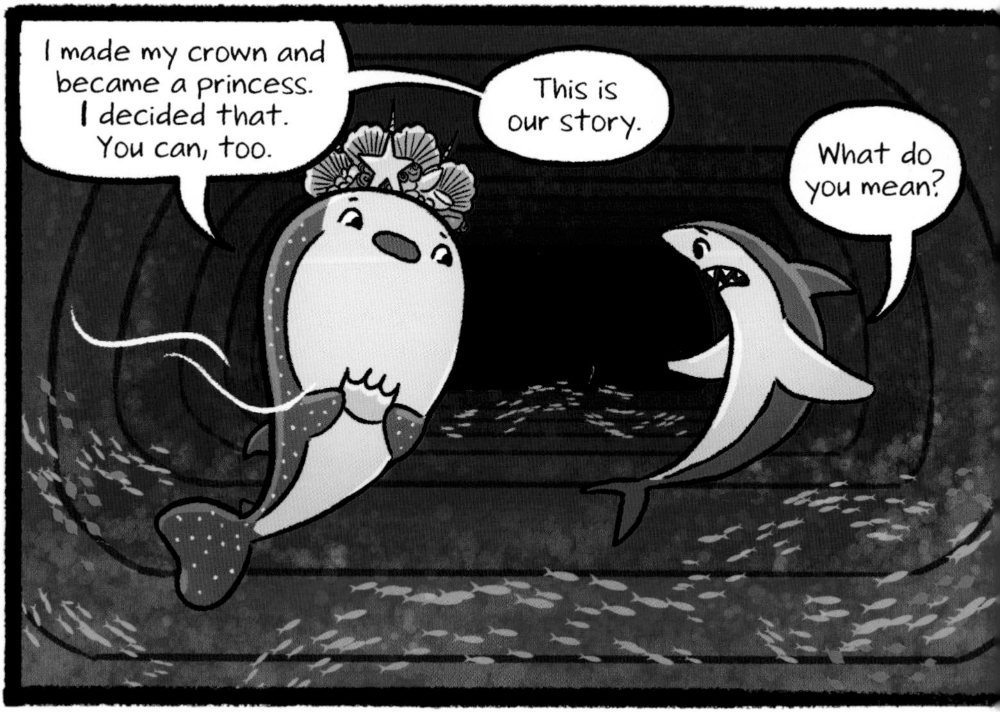
I made my crown and became a princess. I decided that. You can, too.
This is our story.
What do you mean?

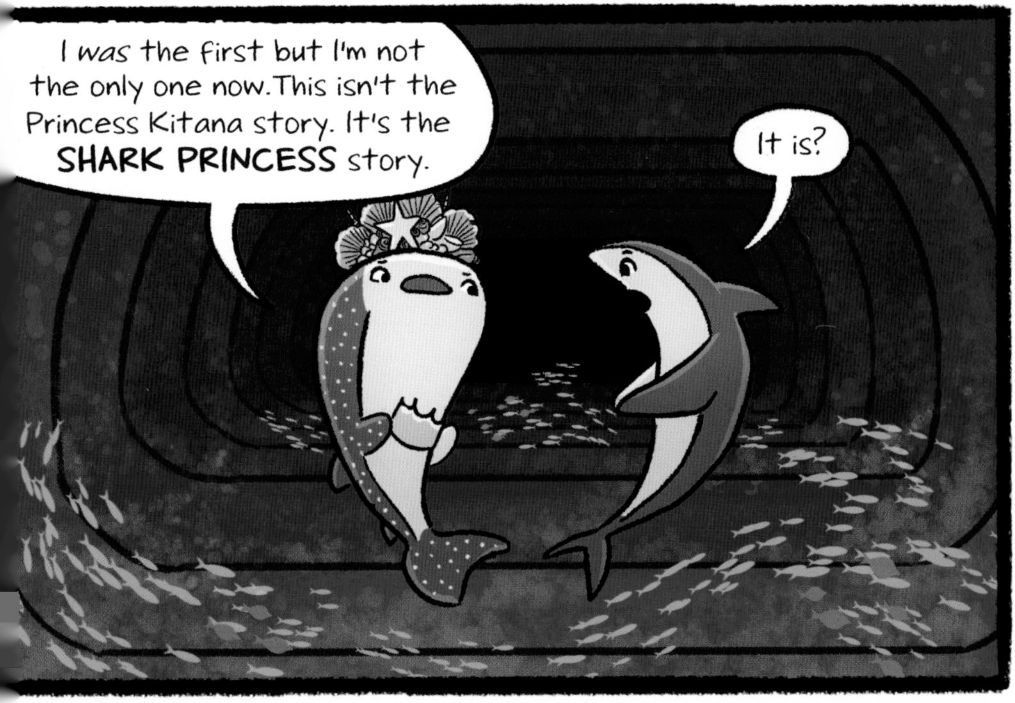
I *was* the first but I'm not the only one now. This isn't the Princess Kitana story. It's the **SHARK PRINCESS** story.
It is?

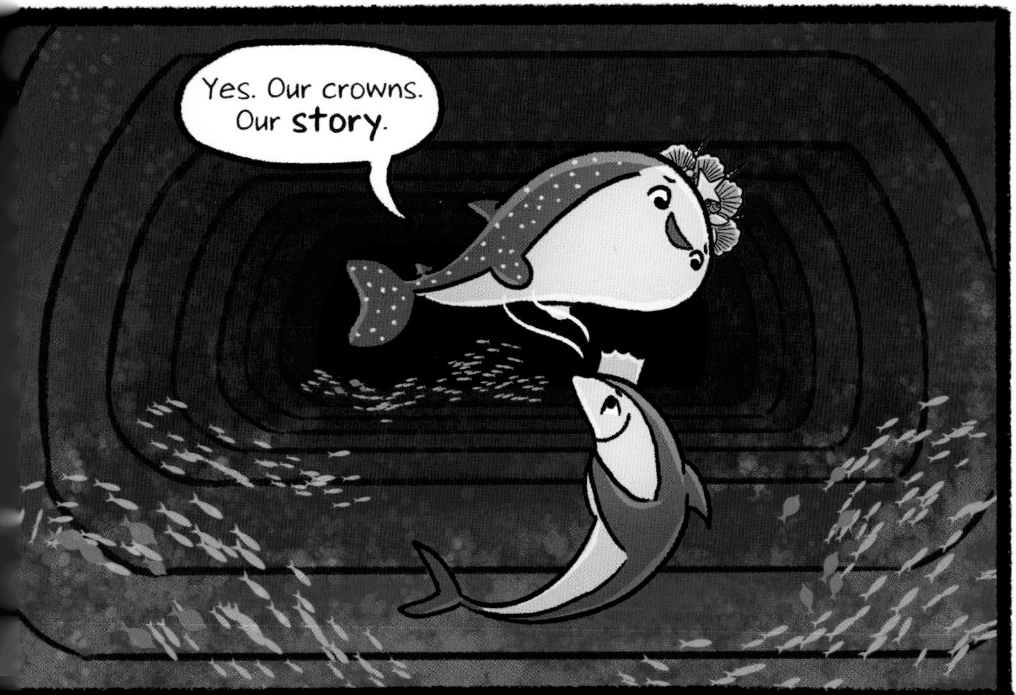
Yes. Our crowns. Our **story**.

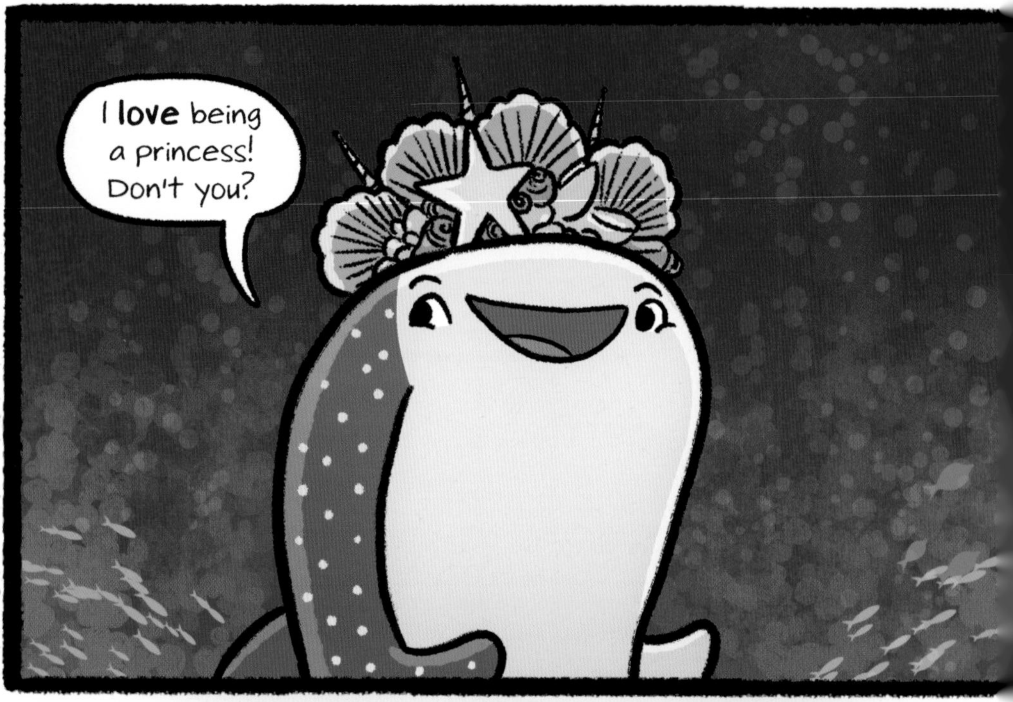
I **love** being a princess! Don't you?

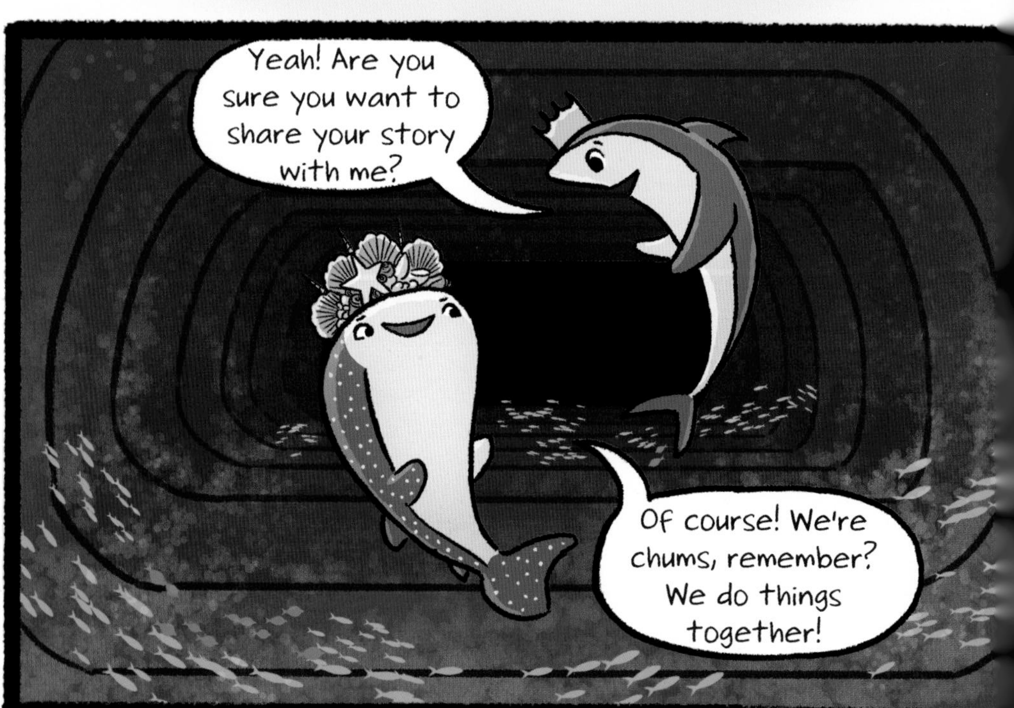
Yeah! Are you sure you want to share your story with me?
Of course! We're chums, remember? We do things together!

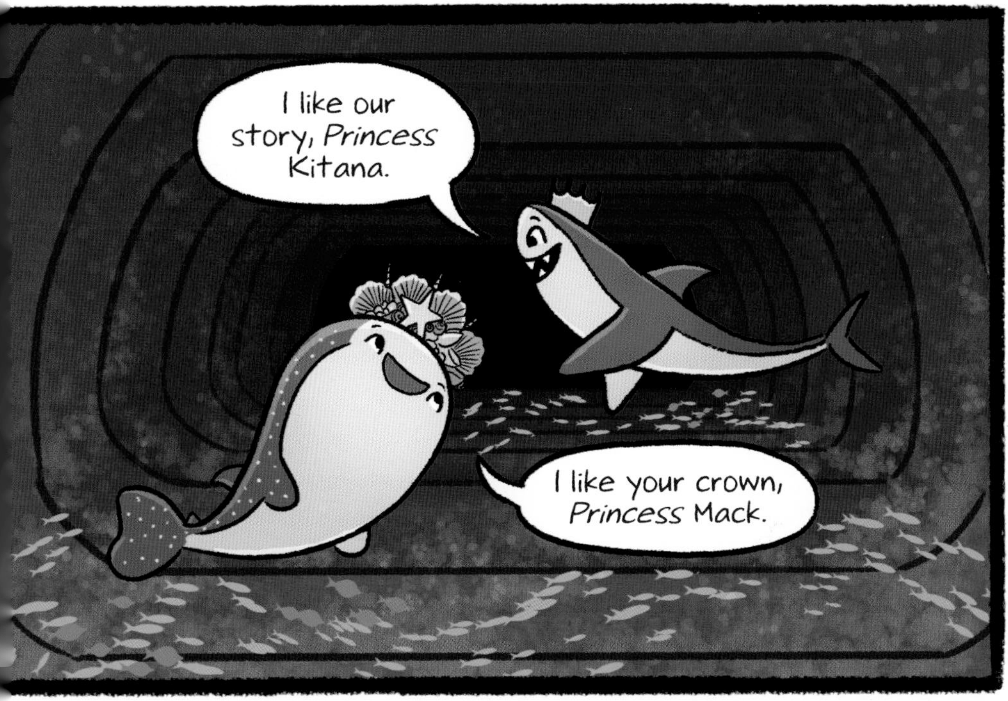
I like our story, *Princess* Kitana.
I like your crown, *Princess* Mack.

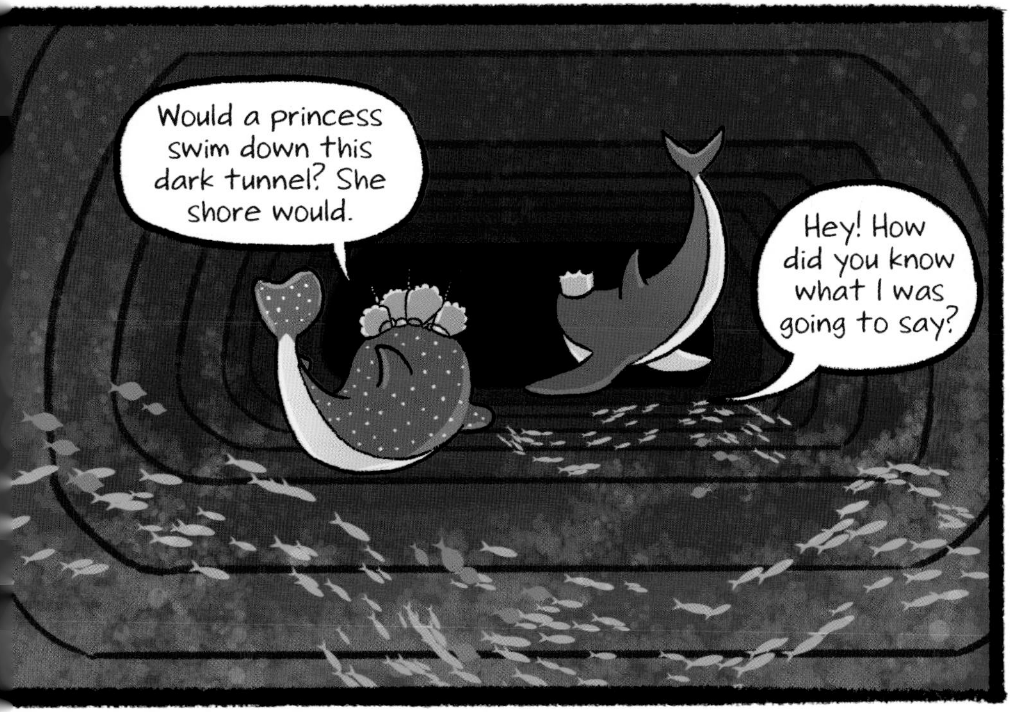
Would a princess swim down this dark tunnel? She shore would.
Hey! How did you know what I was going to say?

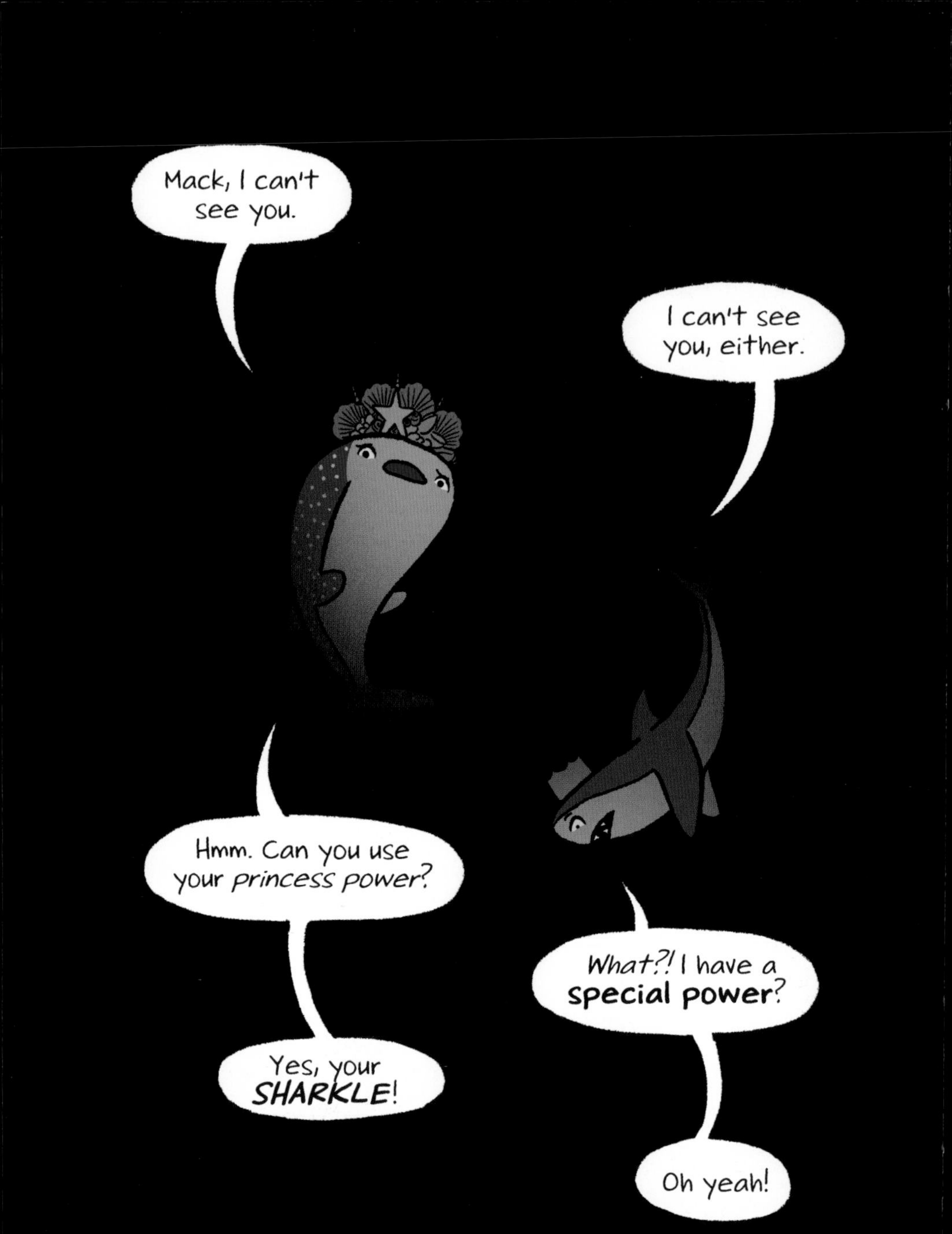
Mack, I can't see you.
I can't see you, either.
Hmm. Can you use your *princess power*?
What?! I have a **special power**?
Yes, your ***SHARKLE***!
Oh yeah!

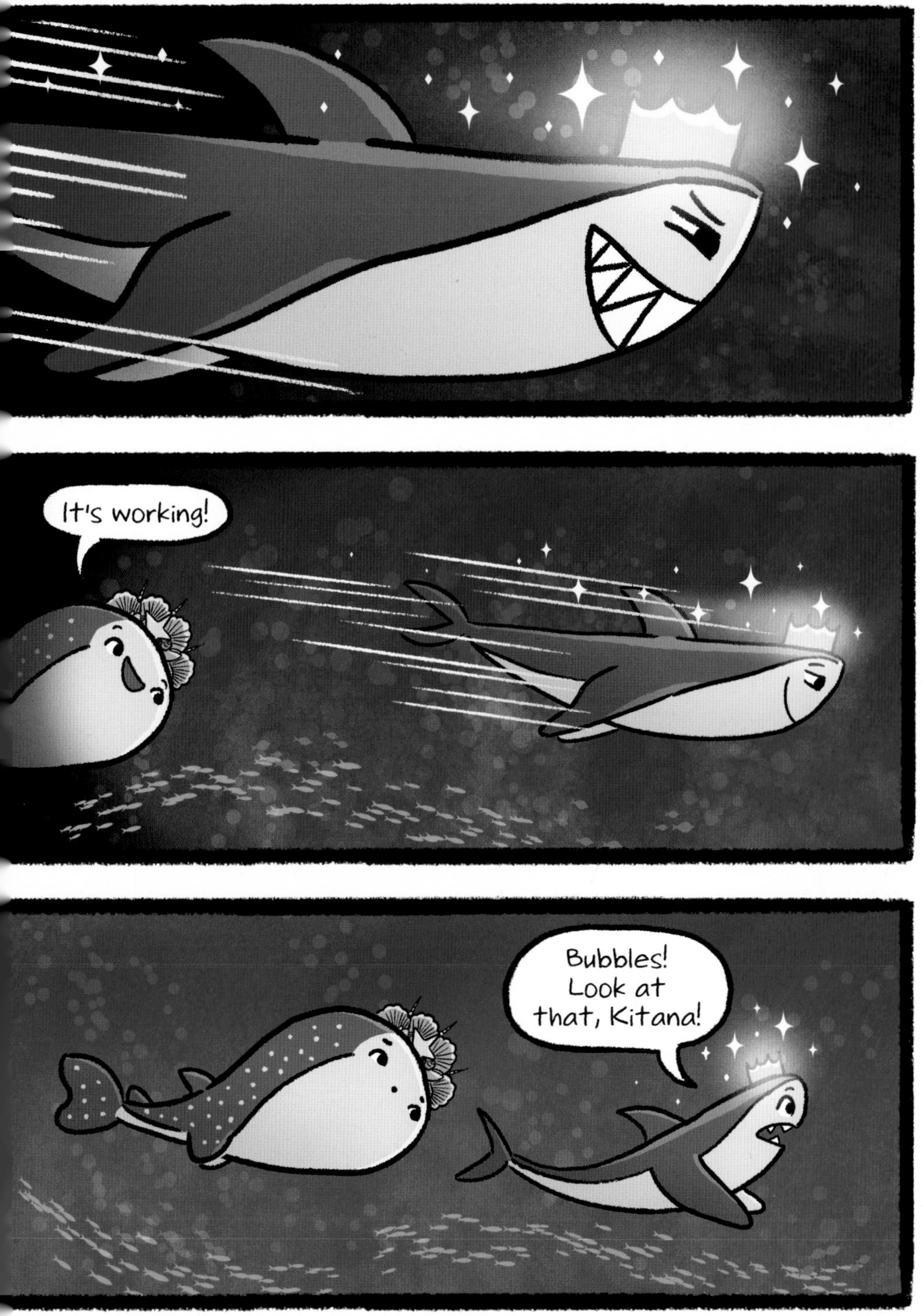
It's working!
Bubbles! Look at that, Kitana!

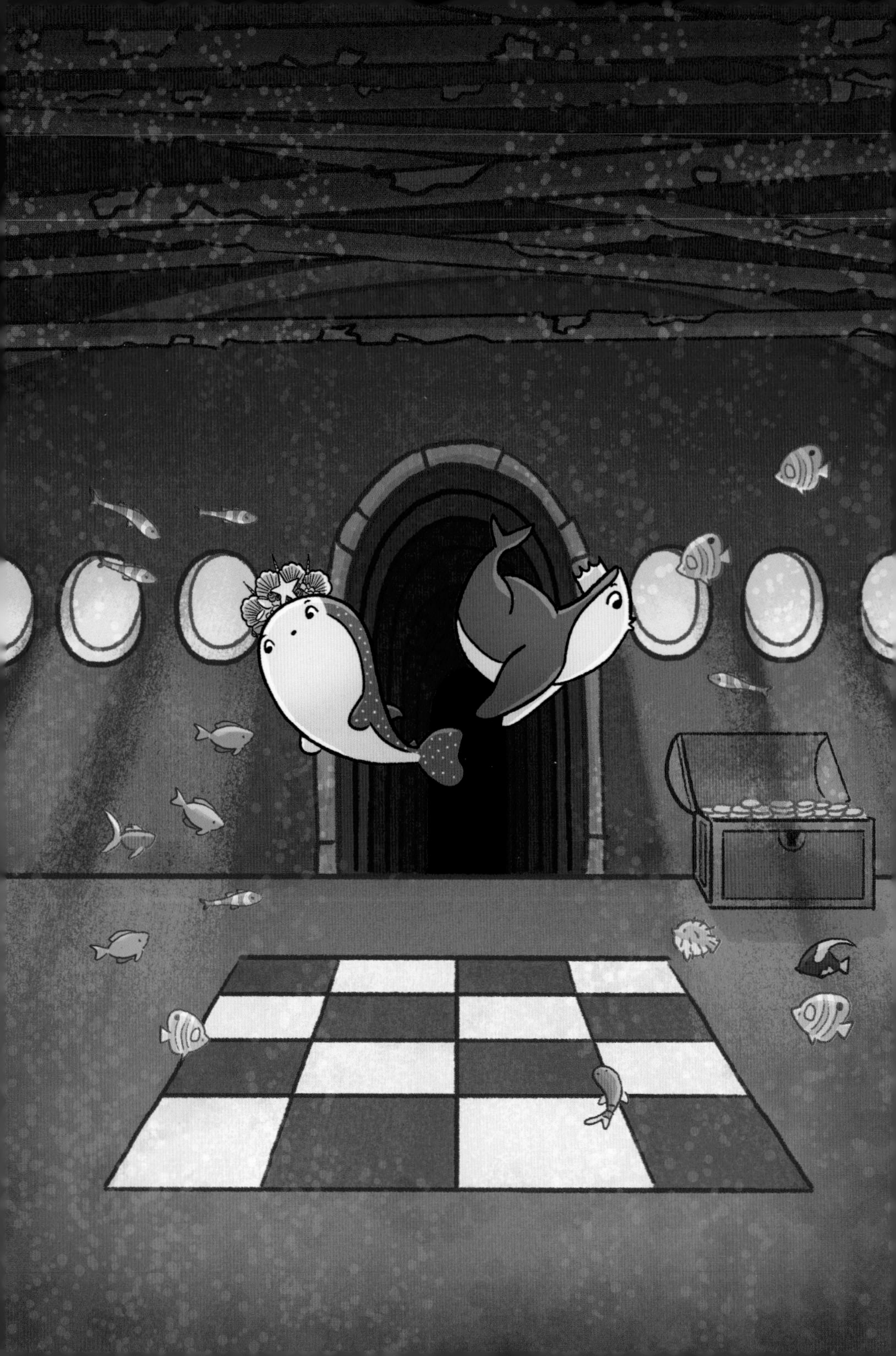

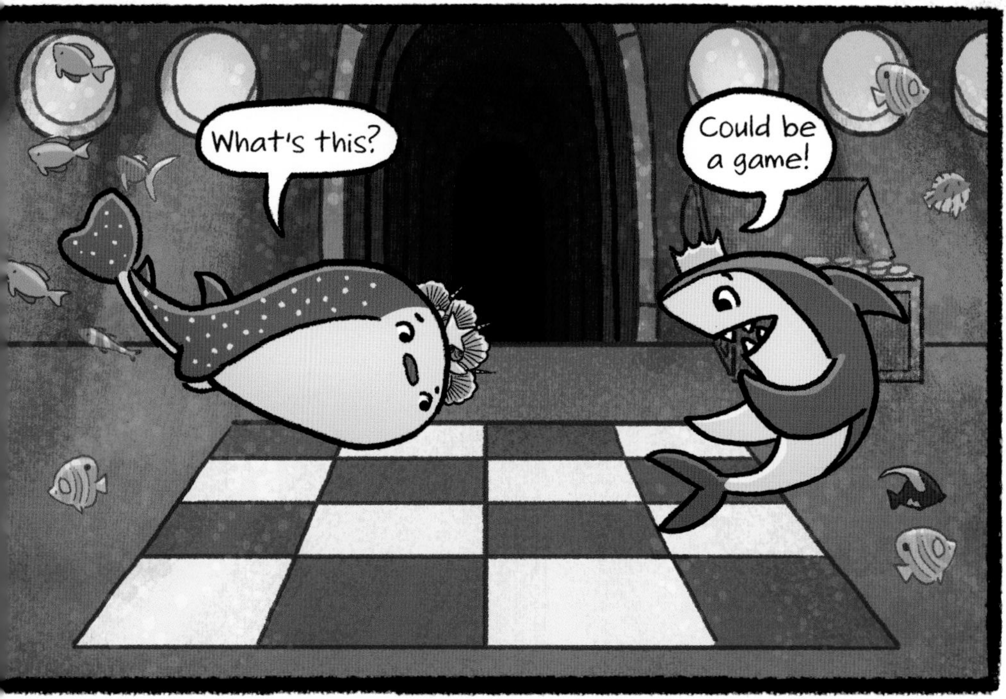
What's this?
Could be a game!

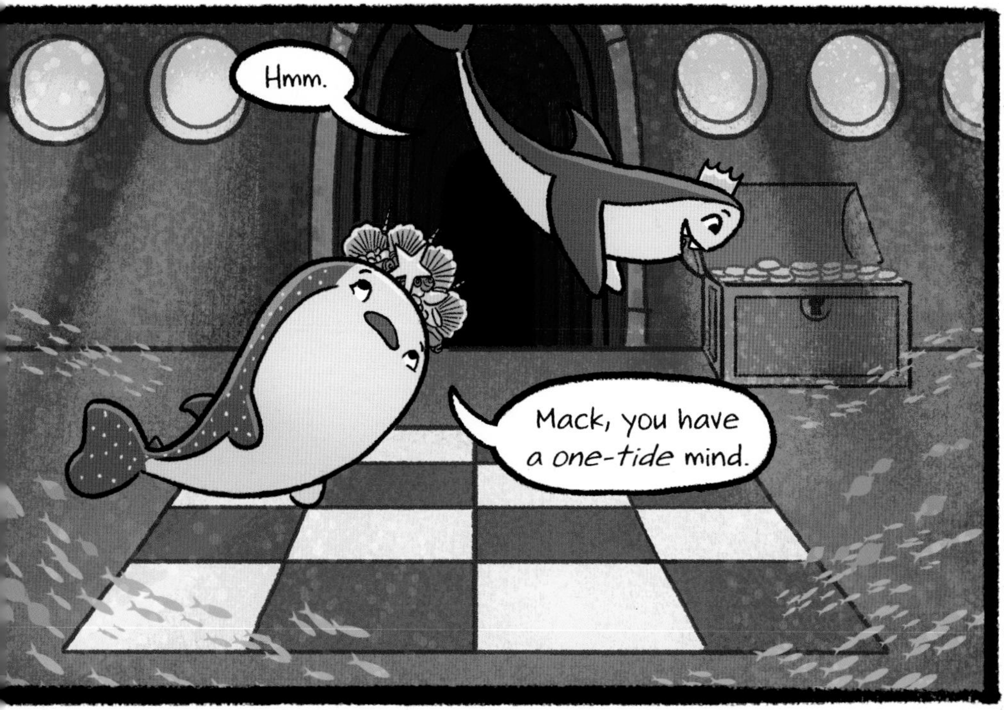
Hmm.
Mack, you have a *one-tide* mind.

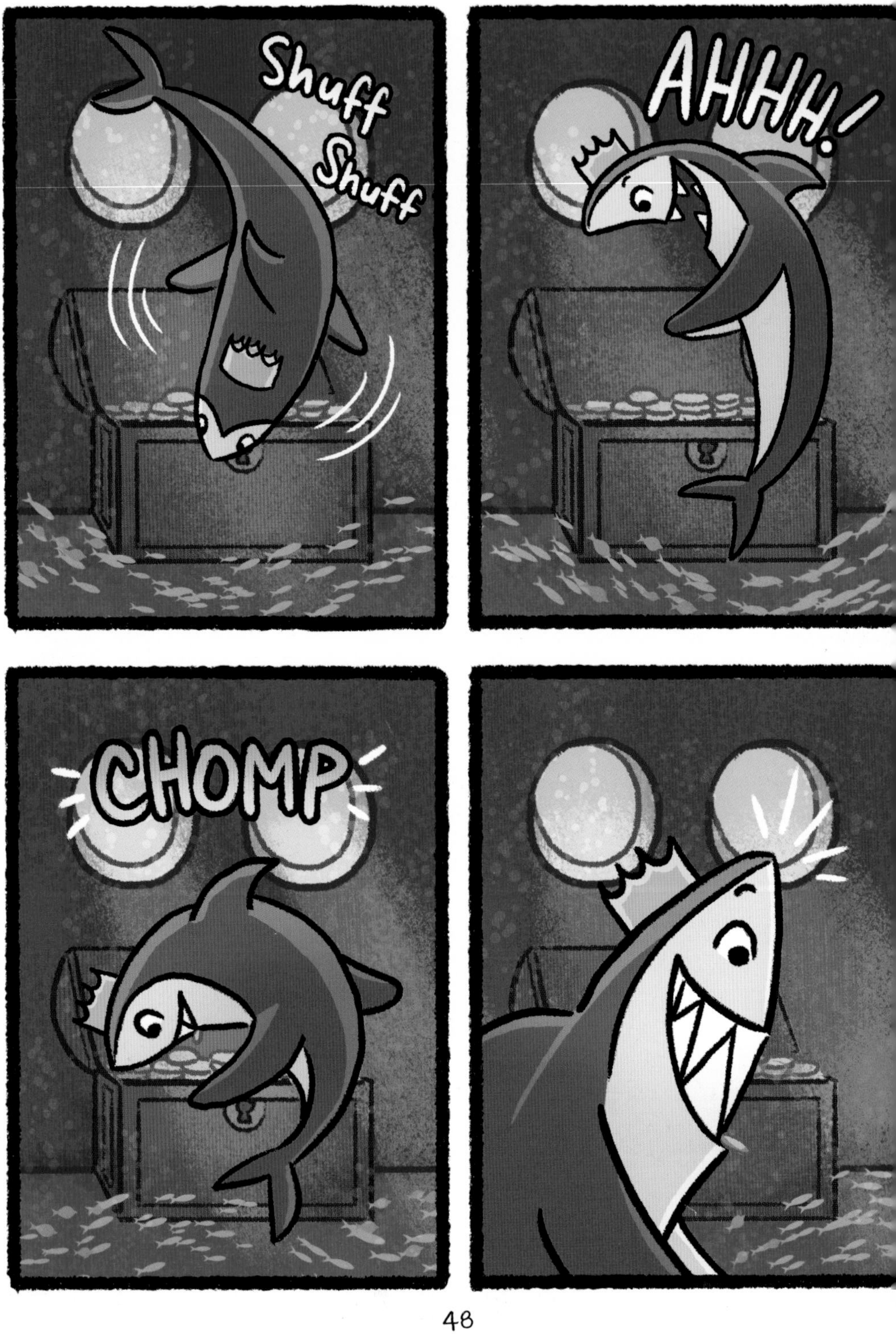
Shuff
Shuff
AHHH!
CHOMP

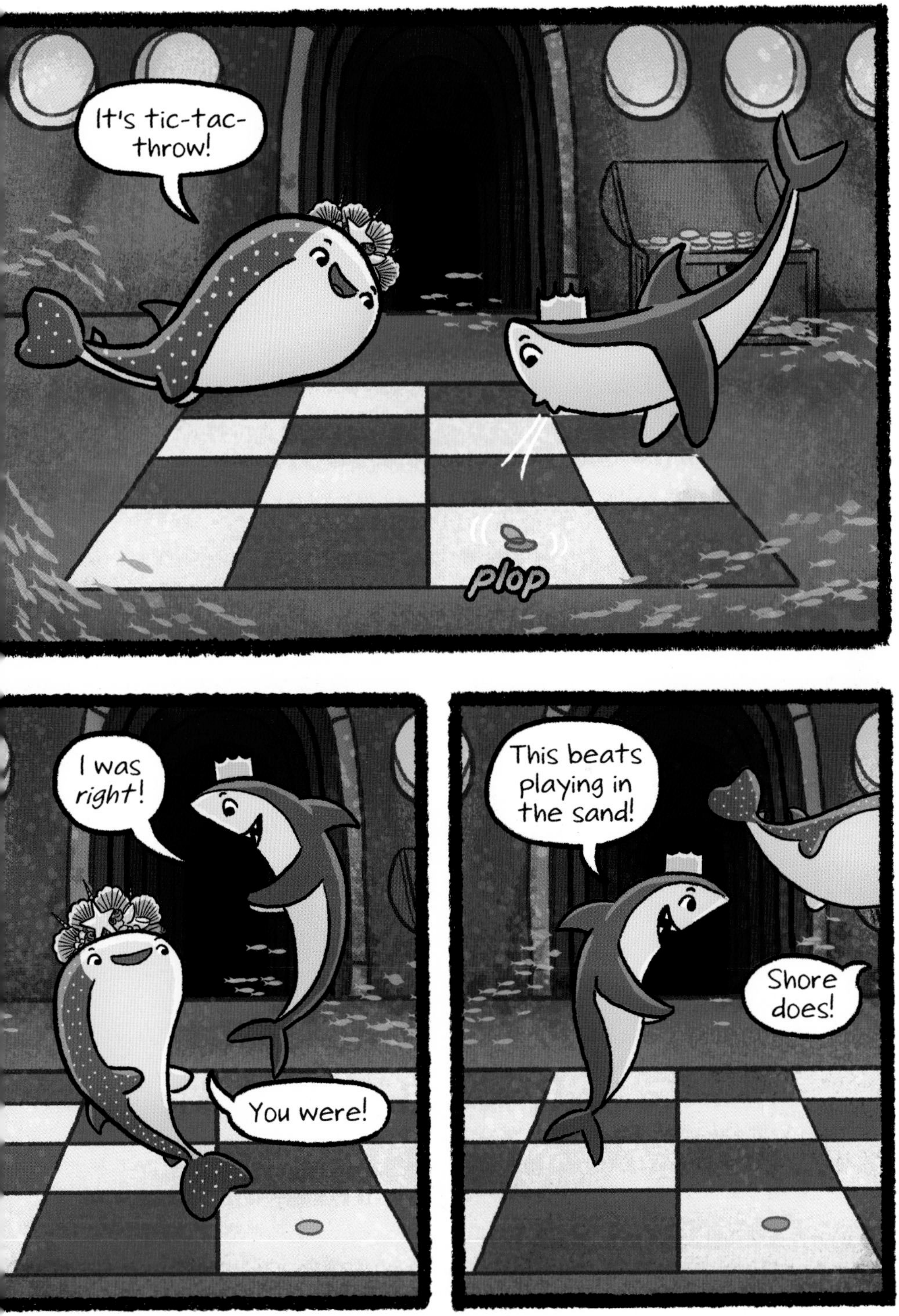
It's tic-tac-throw!
plop
I was right!
You were!
This beats playing in the sand!
Shore does!

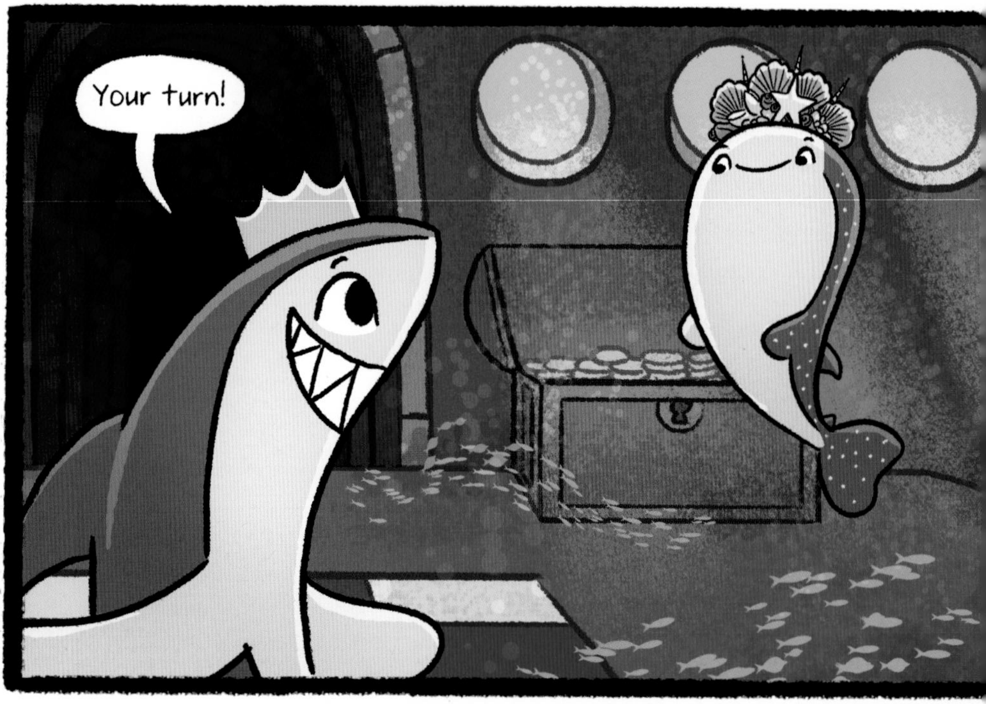
Your turn!

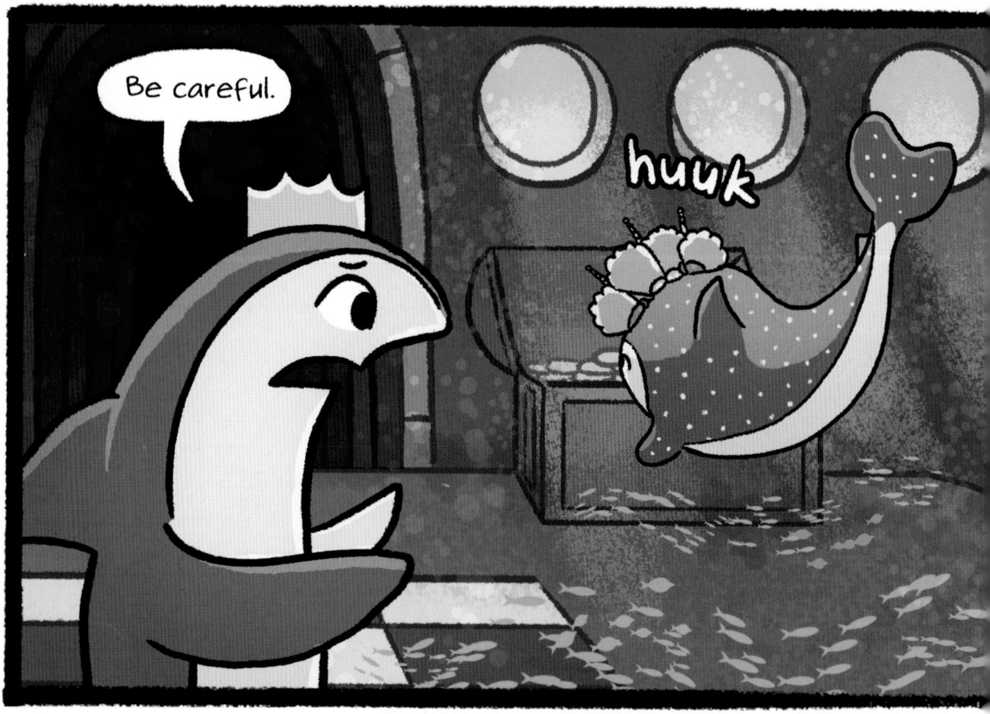
Be careful.
huuk

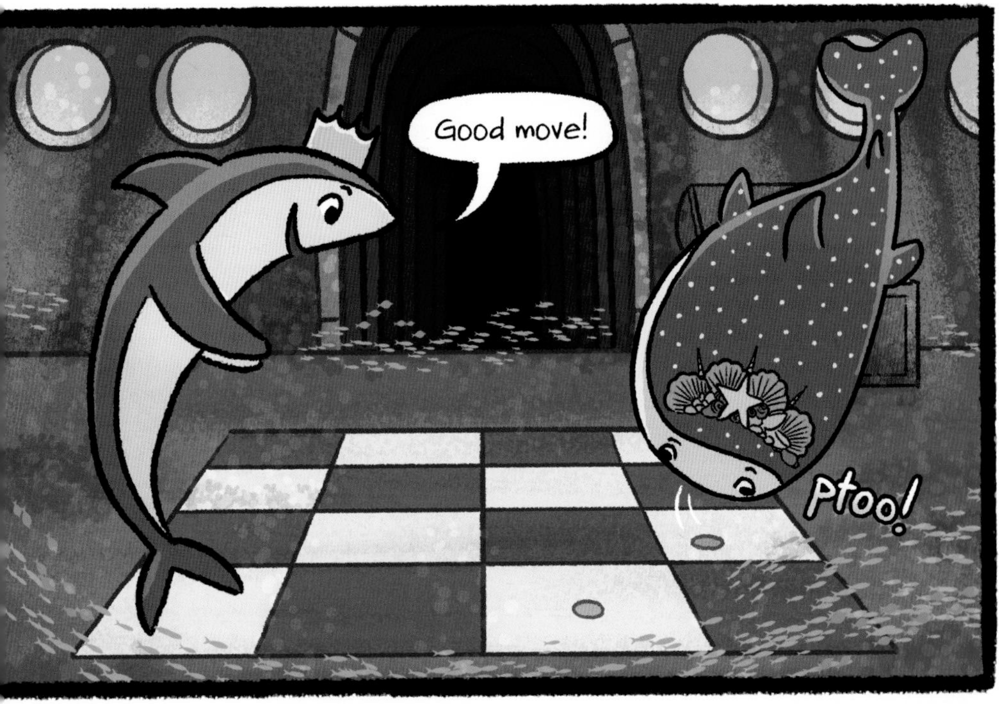
Good move!
Ptoo!

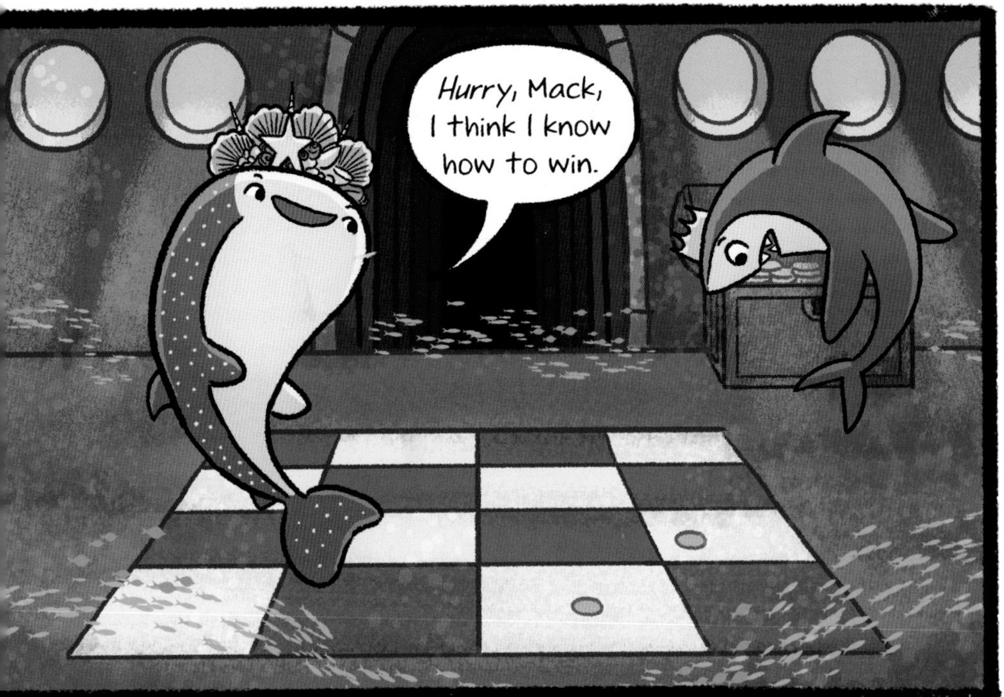
Hurry, Mack, I think I know how to win.

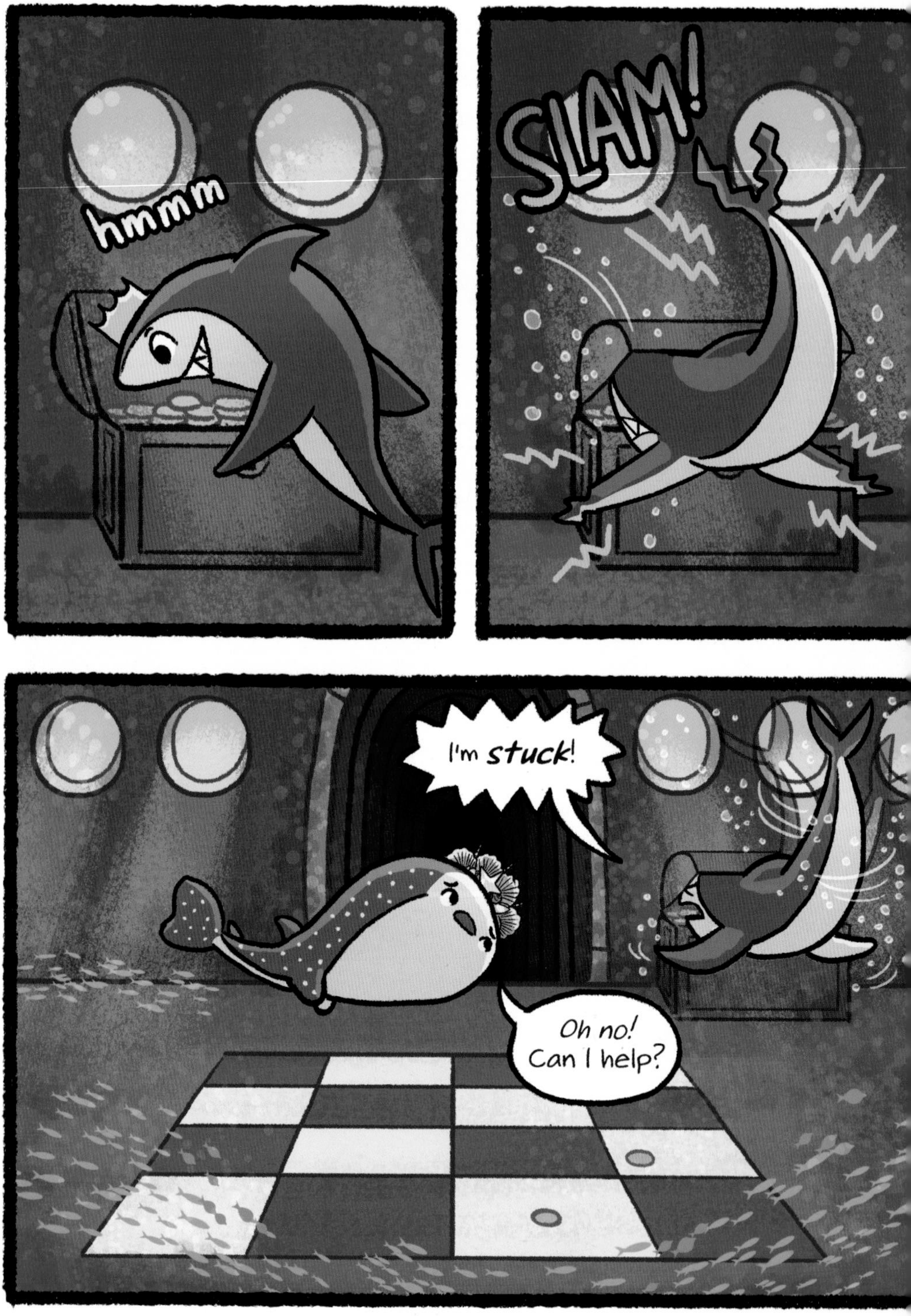
hmmm
SLAM!
I'm stuck!
Oh no! Can I help?

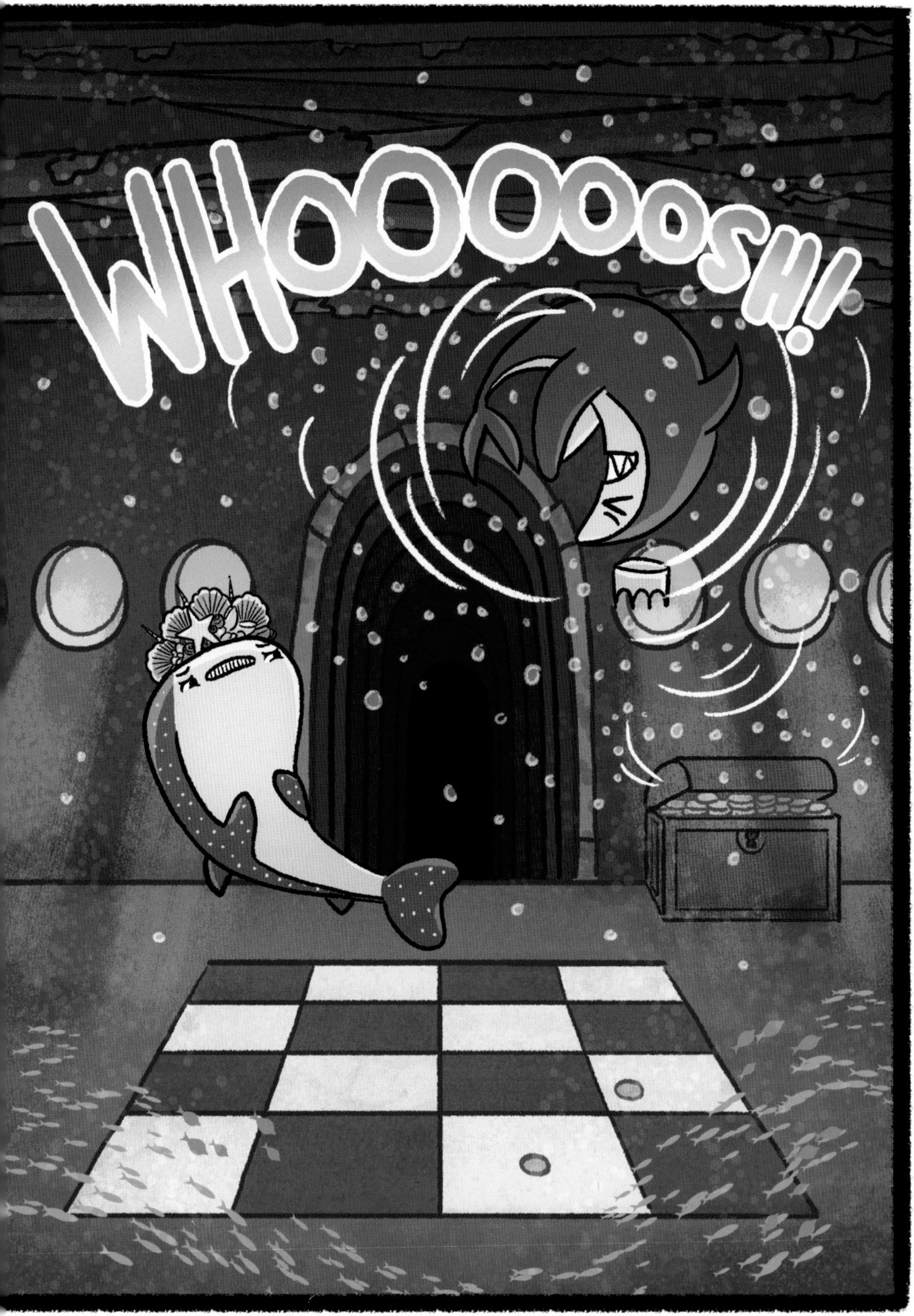
WHOOOOOOSH!!

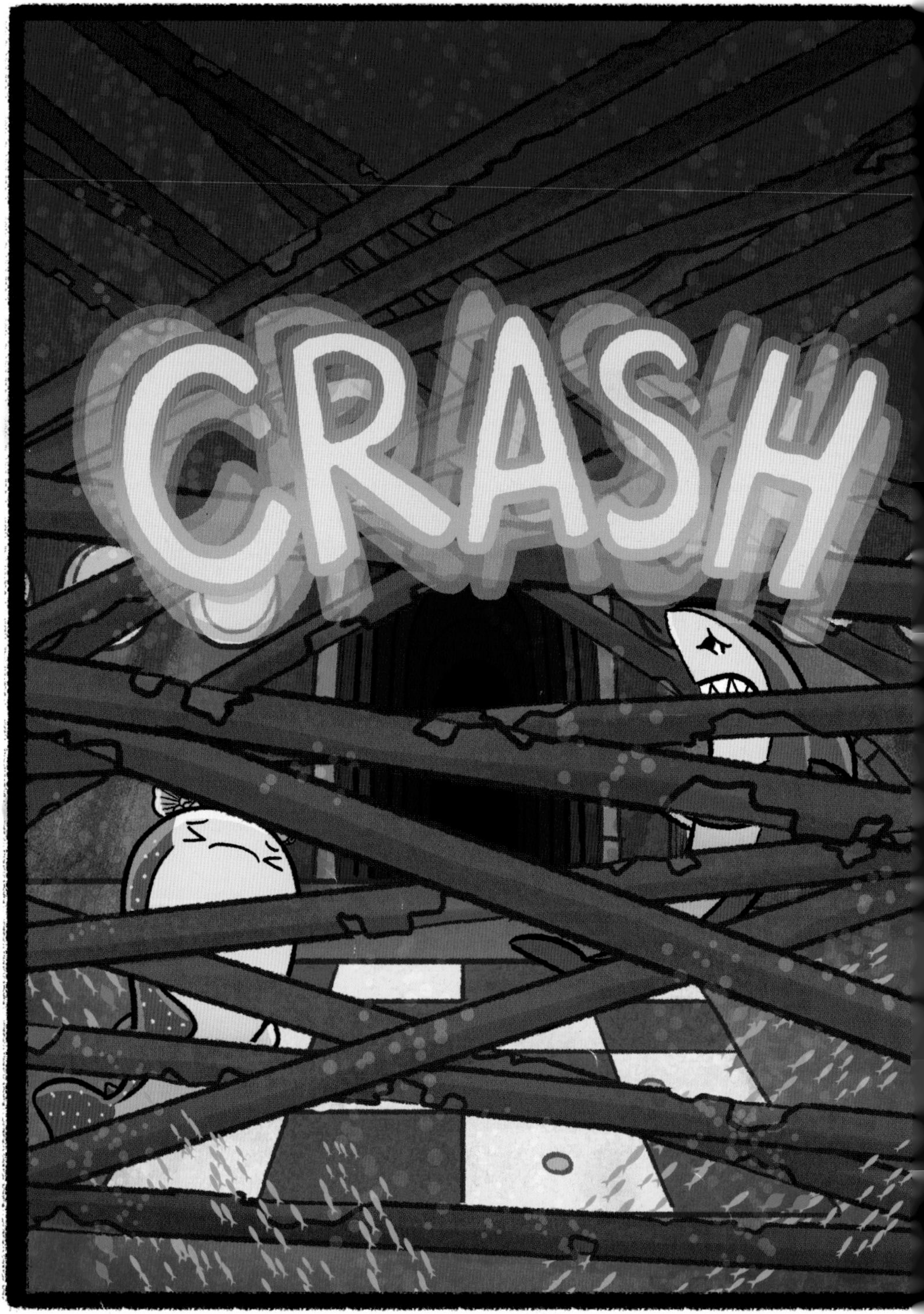
CRASH

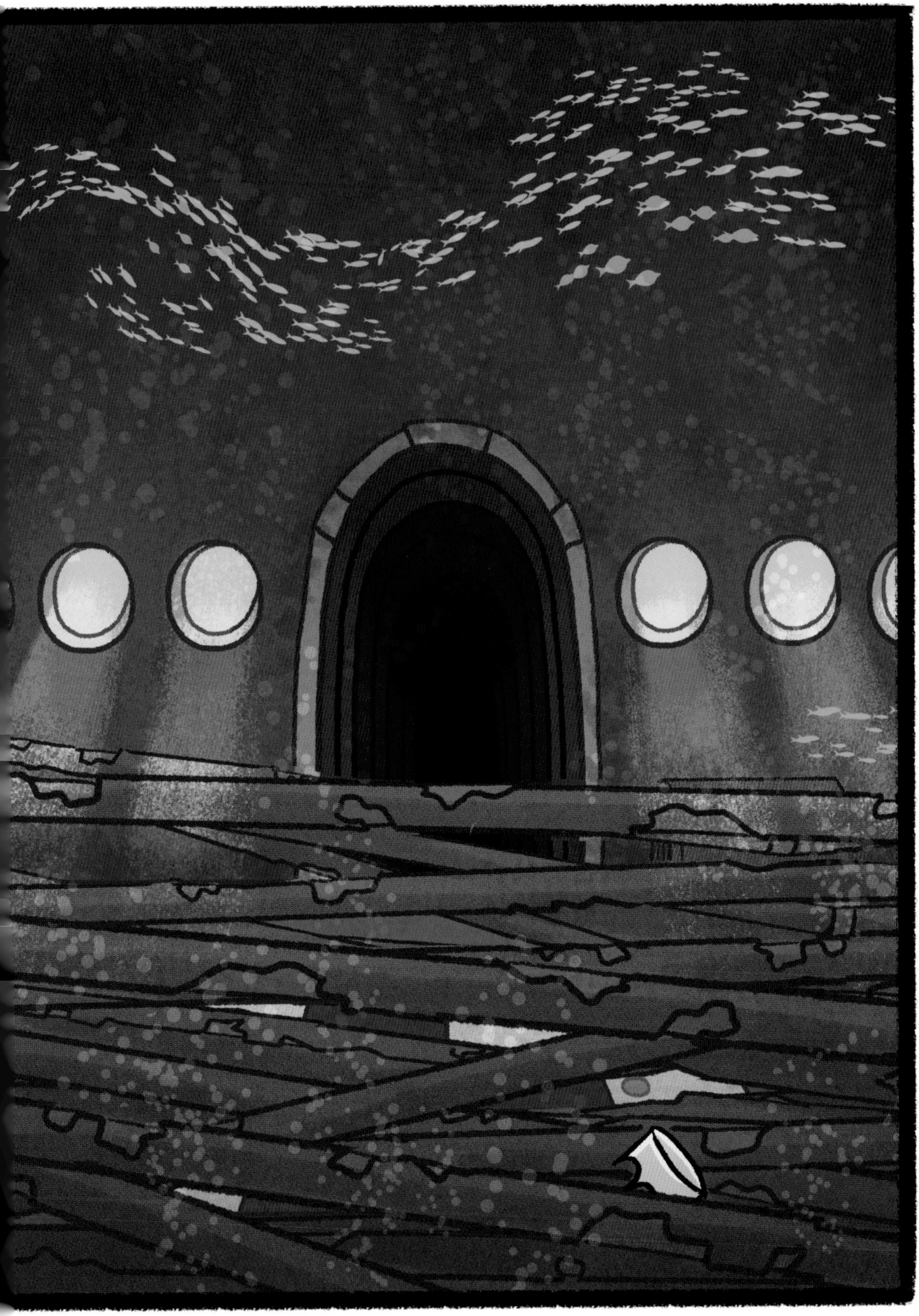

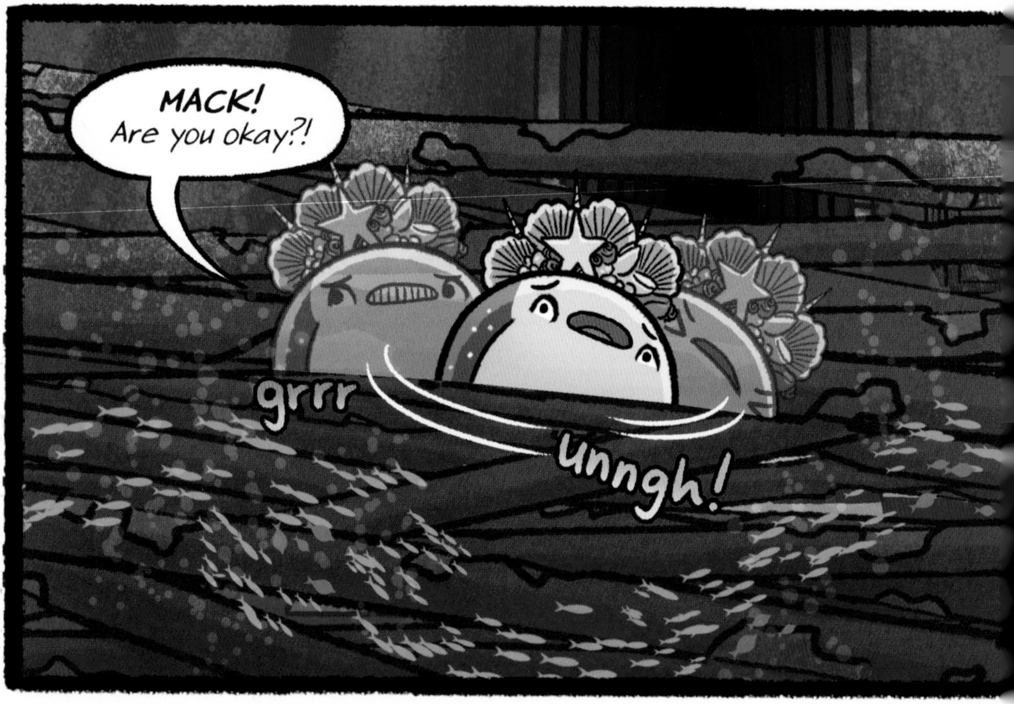
MACK!
Are you okay?!
grrr
unngh!

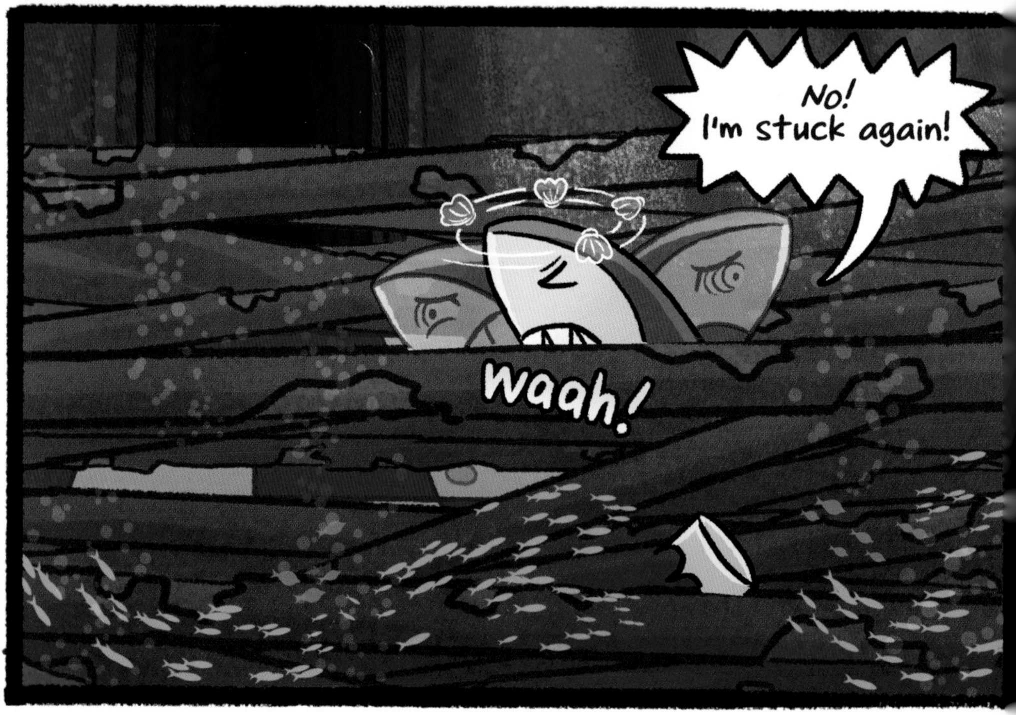
No!
I'm stuck again!
Waah!

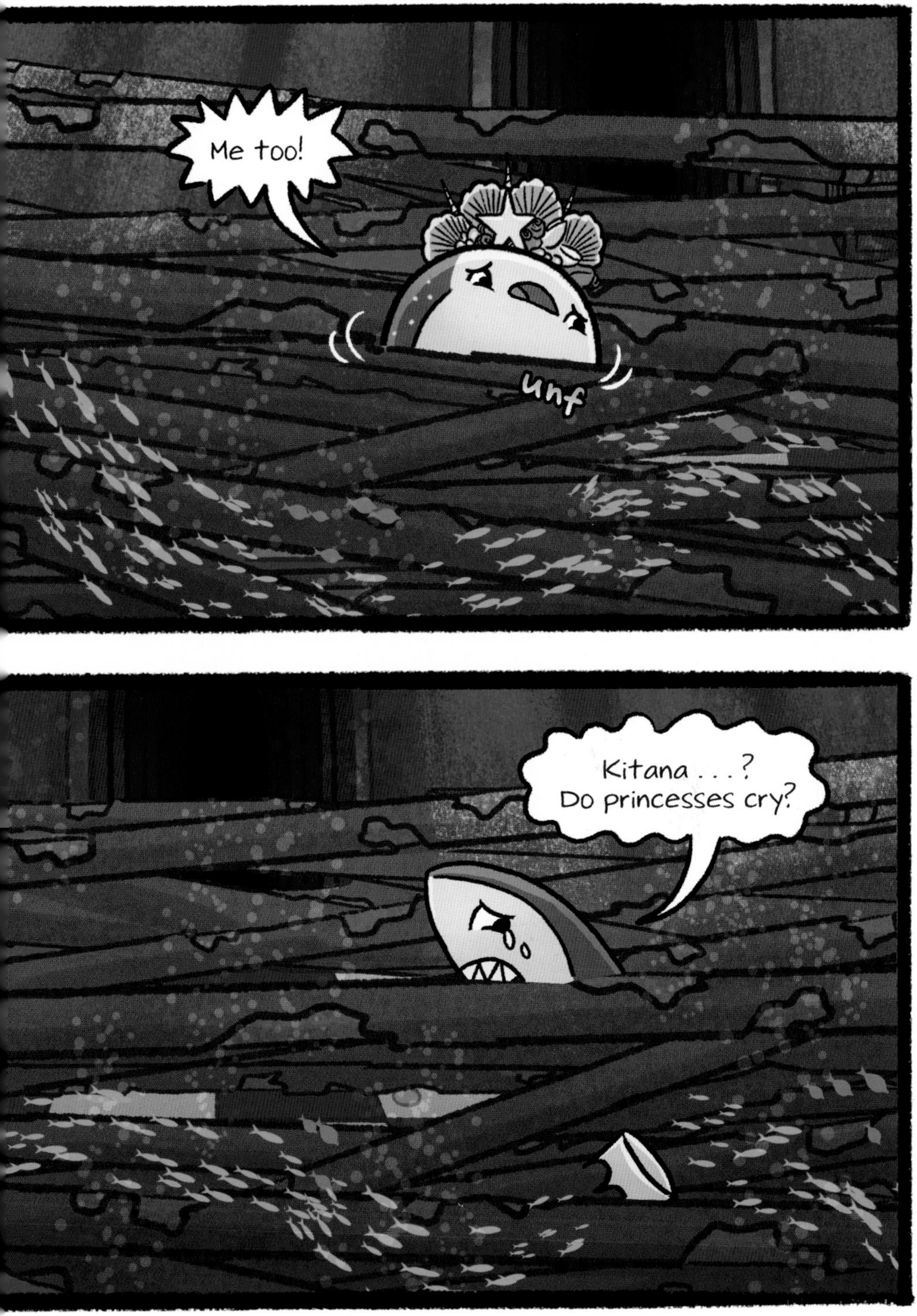
Me too!
unf
Kitana . . . ?
Do princesses cry?

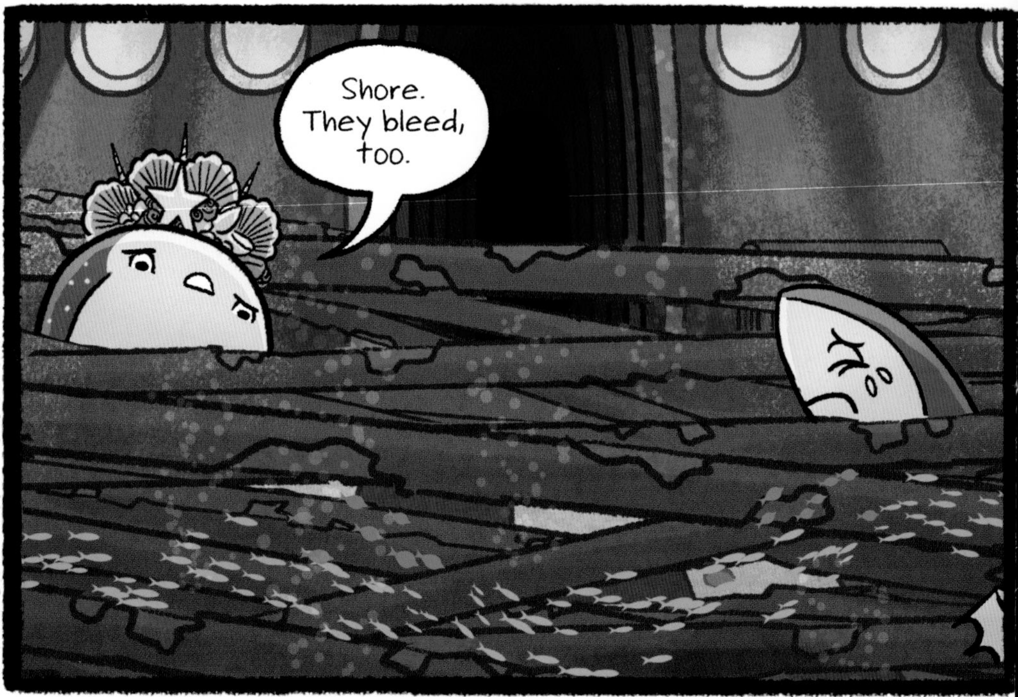
Shore. They bleed, too.

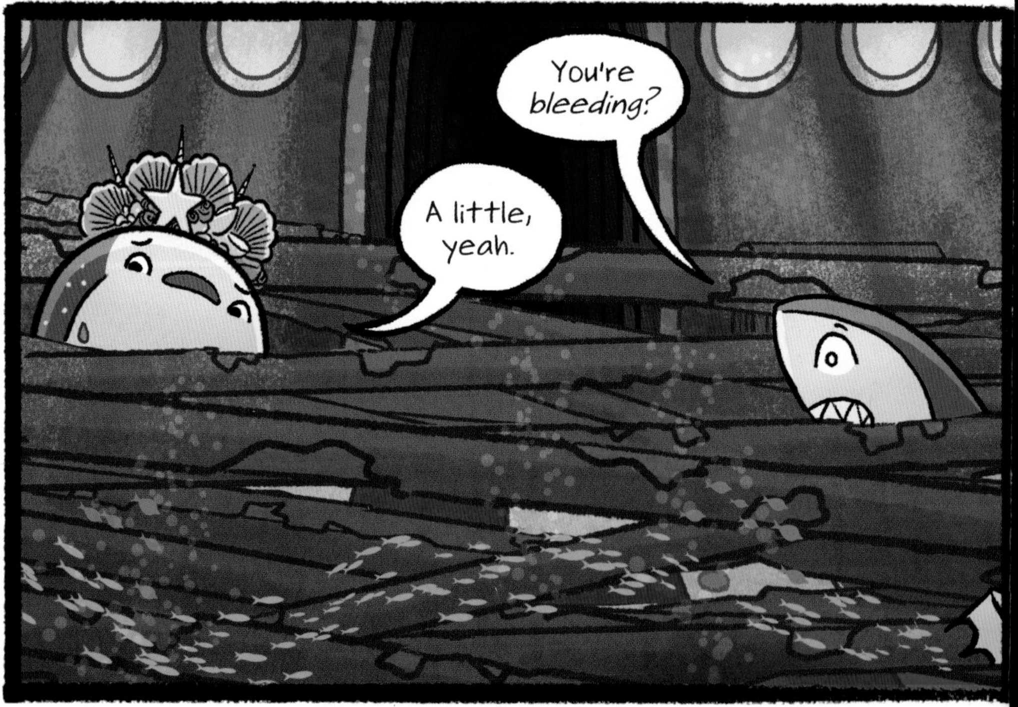
You're bleeding?
A little, yeah.

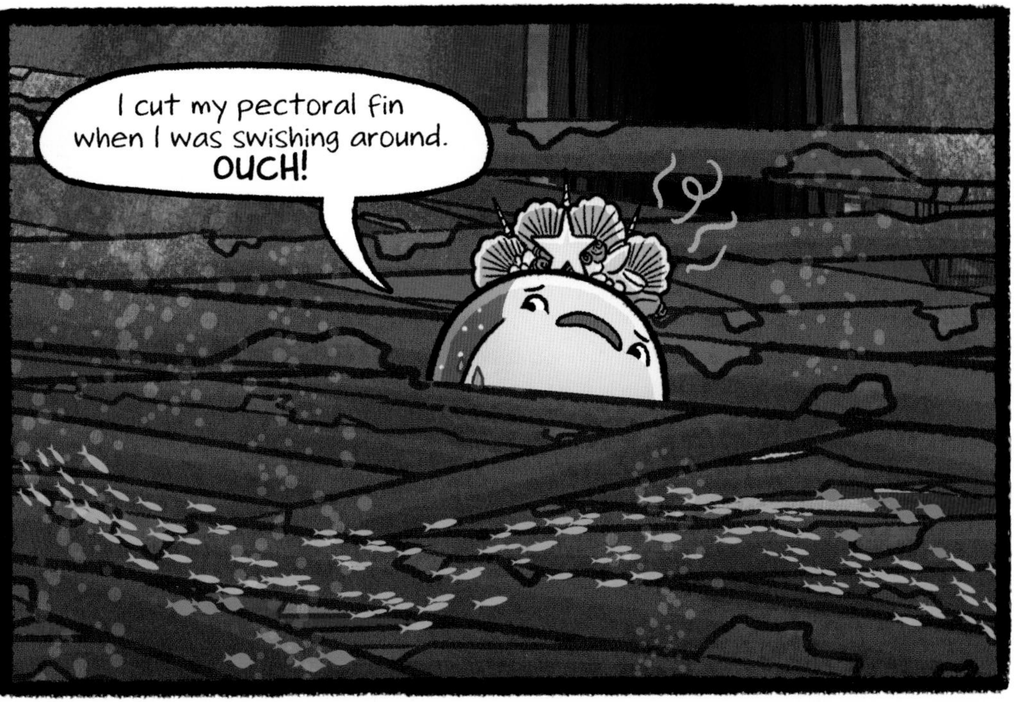
I cut my pectoral fin when I was swishing around. **OUCH!**

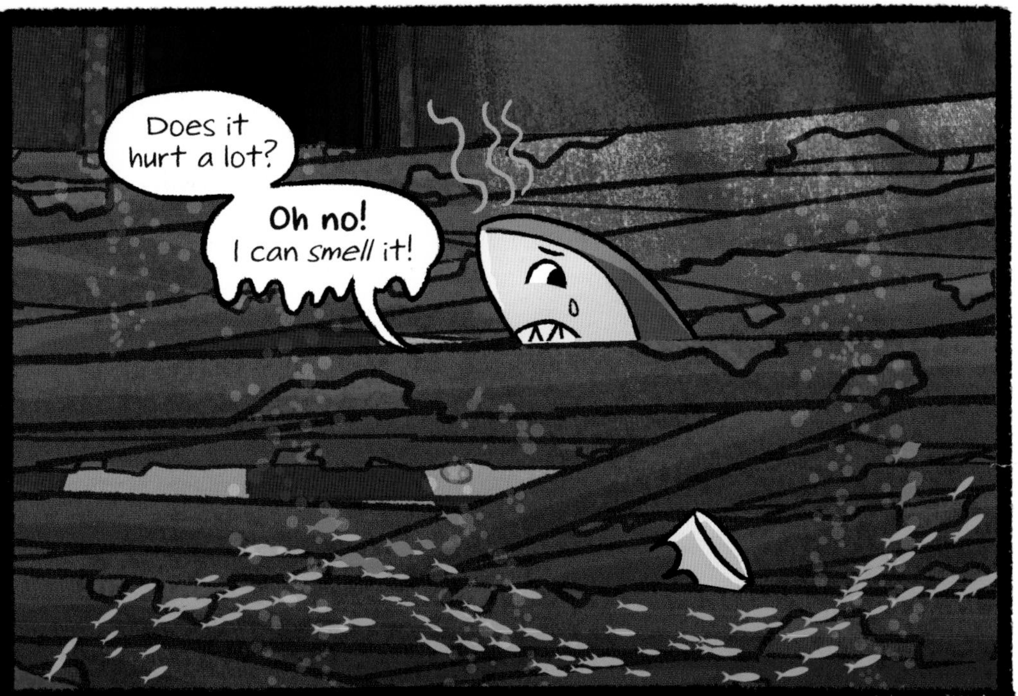
Does it hurt a lot?
Oh no! I can *smell* it!

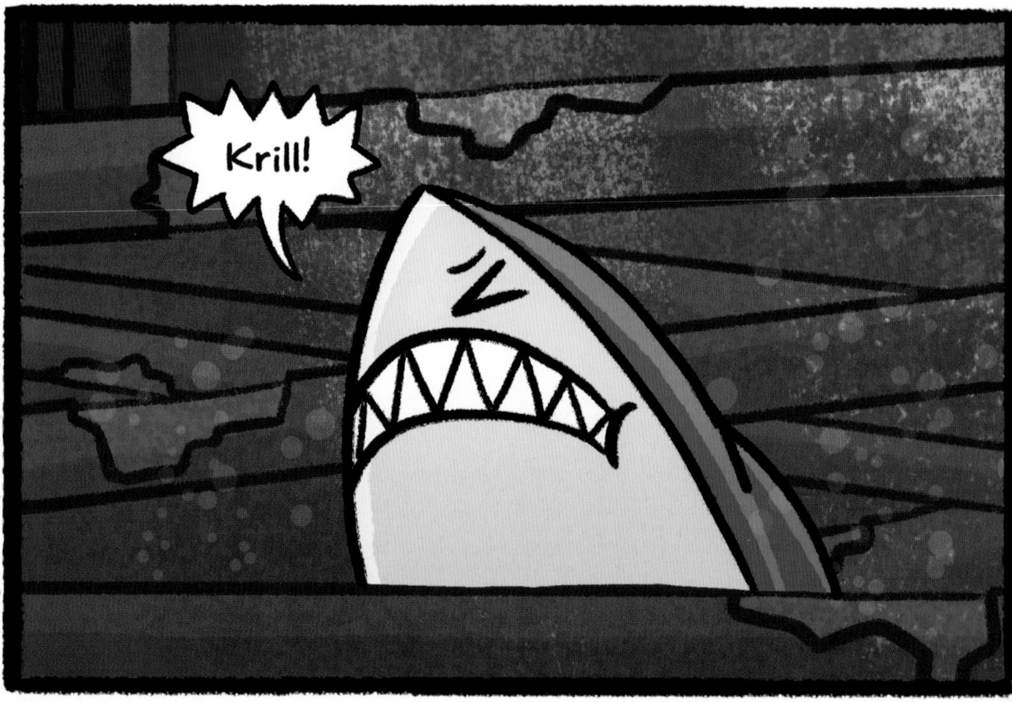
Krill!

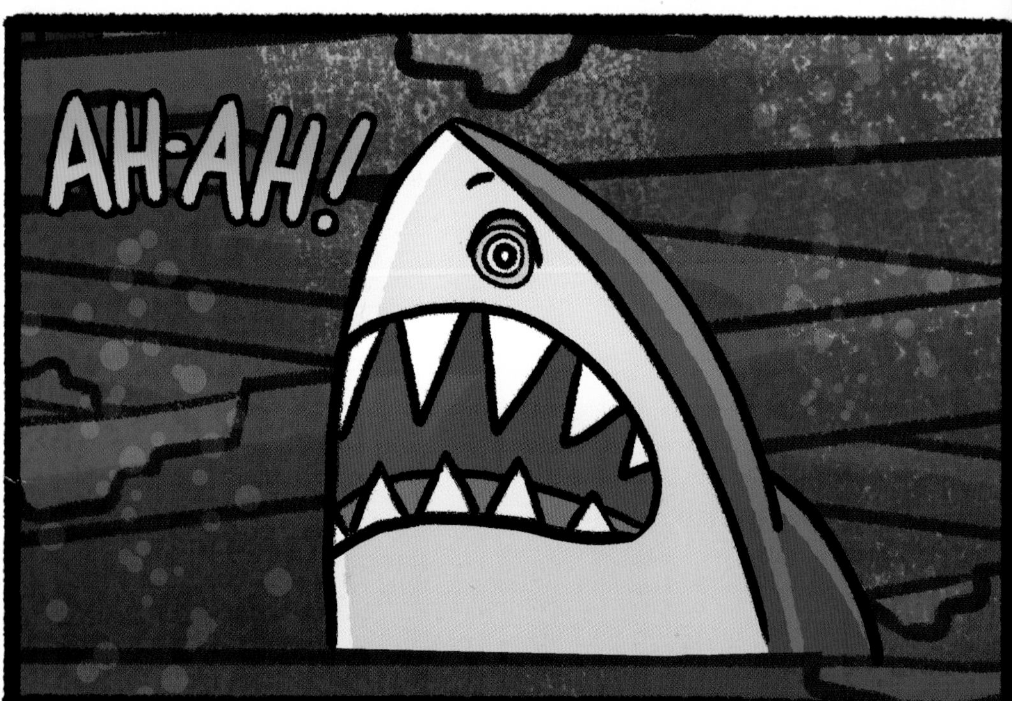
AH-AH!

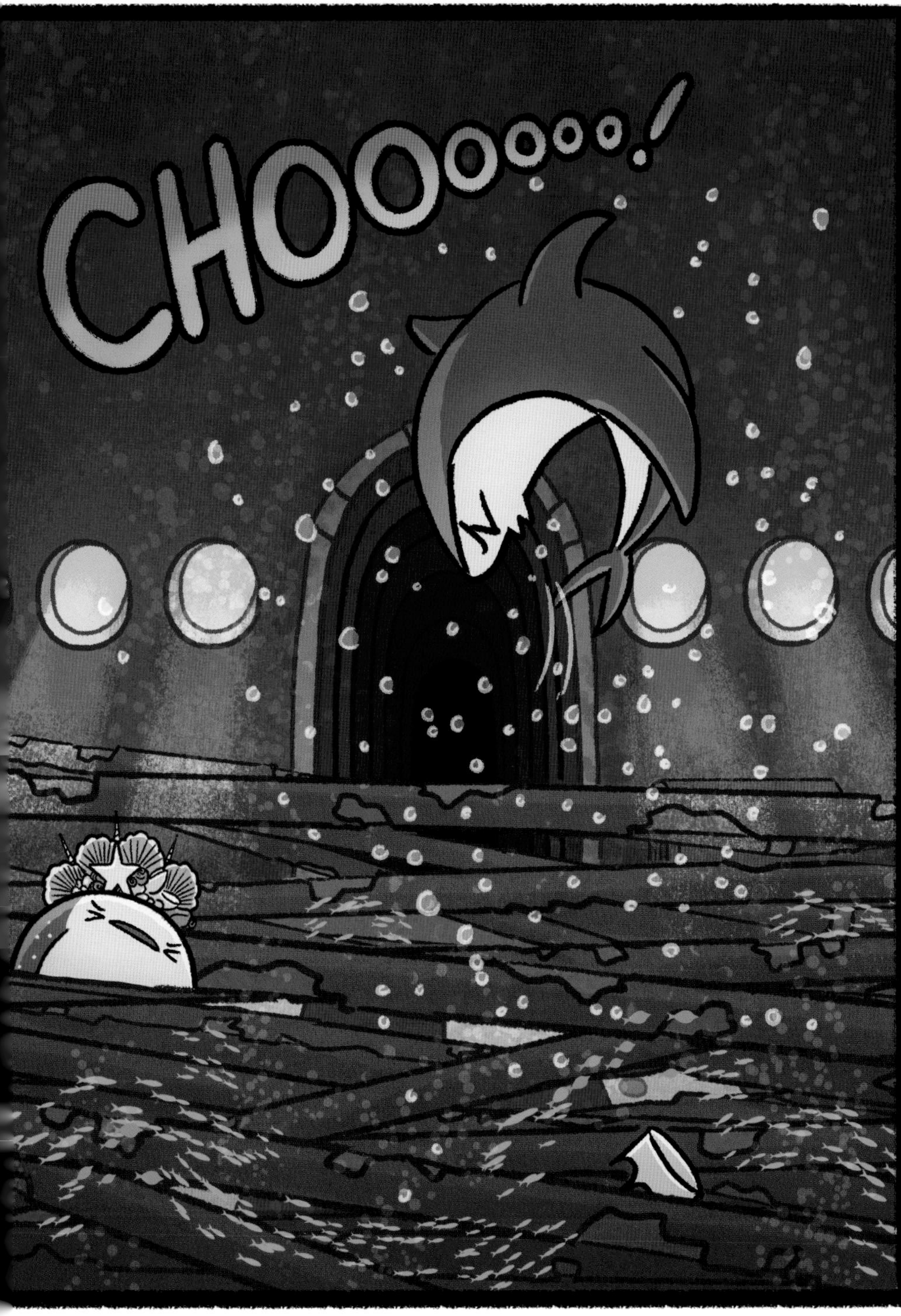
CHOOoooo!

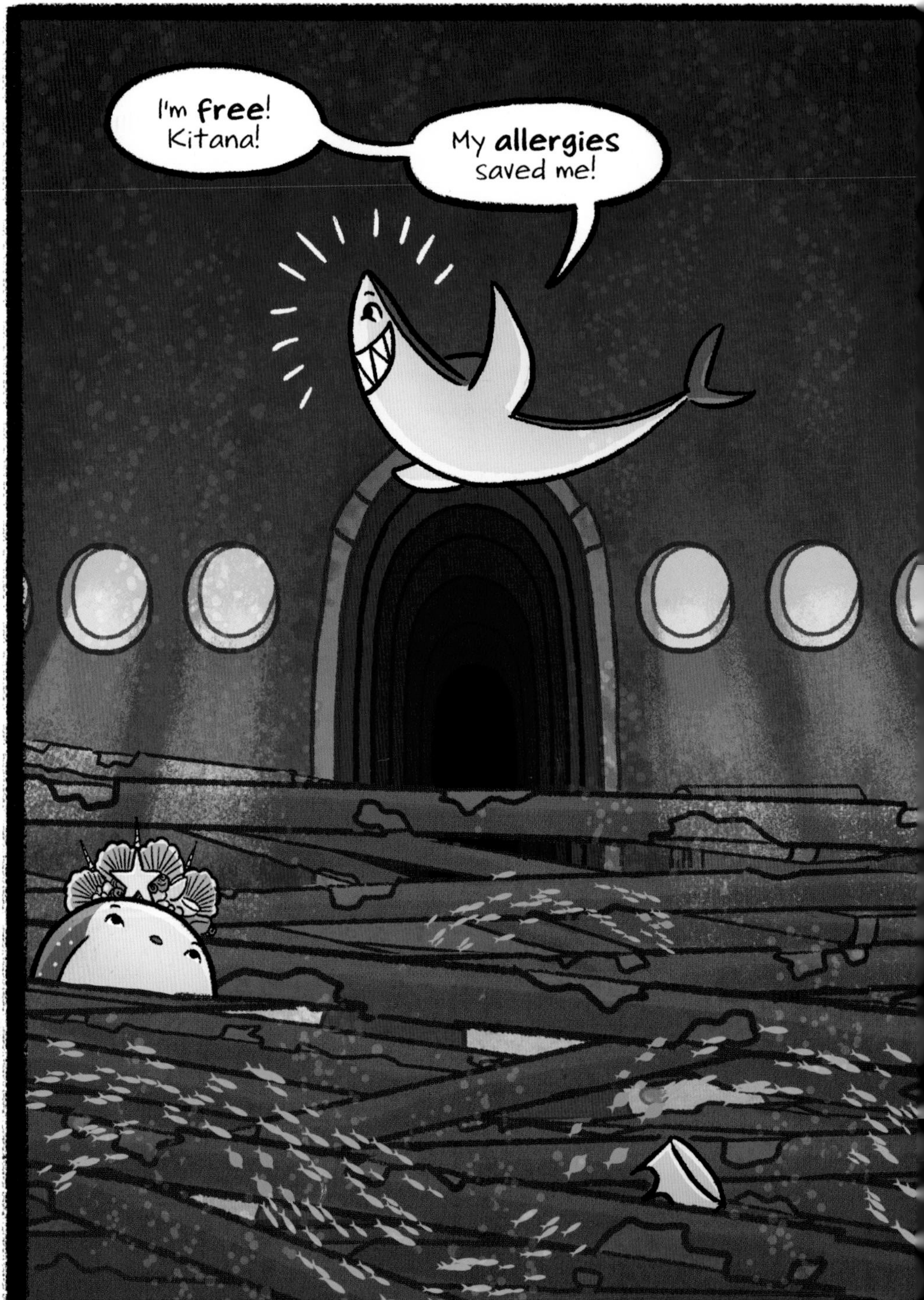
I'm free! Kitana!
My allergies saved me!

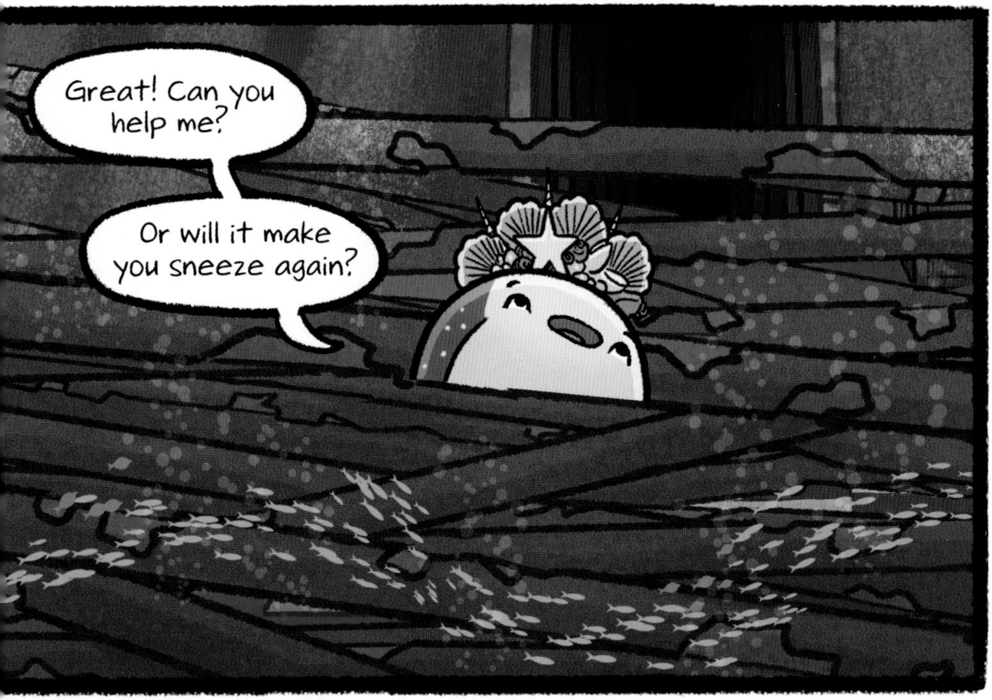

Great! Can you help me?
Or will it make you sneeze again?

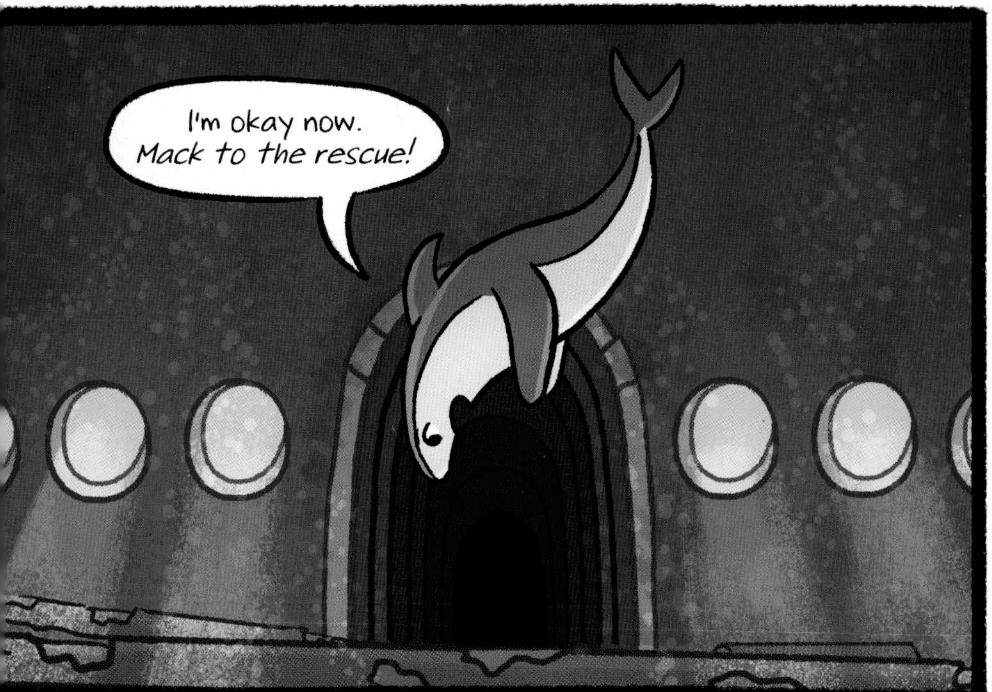

I'm okay now. Mack to the rescue!

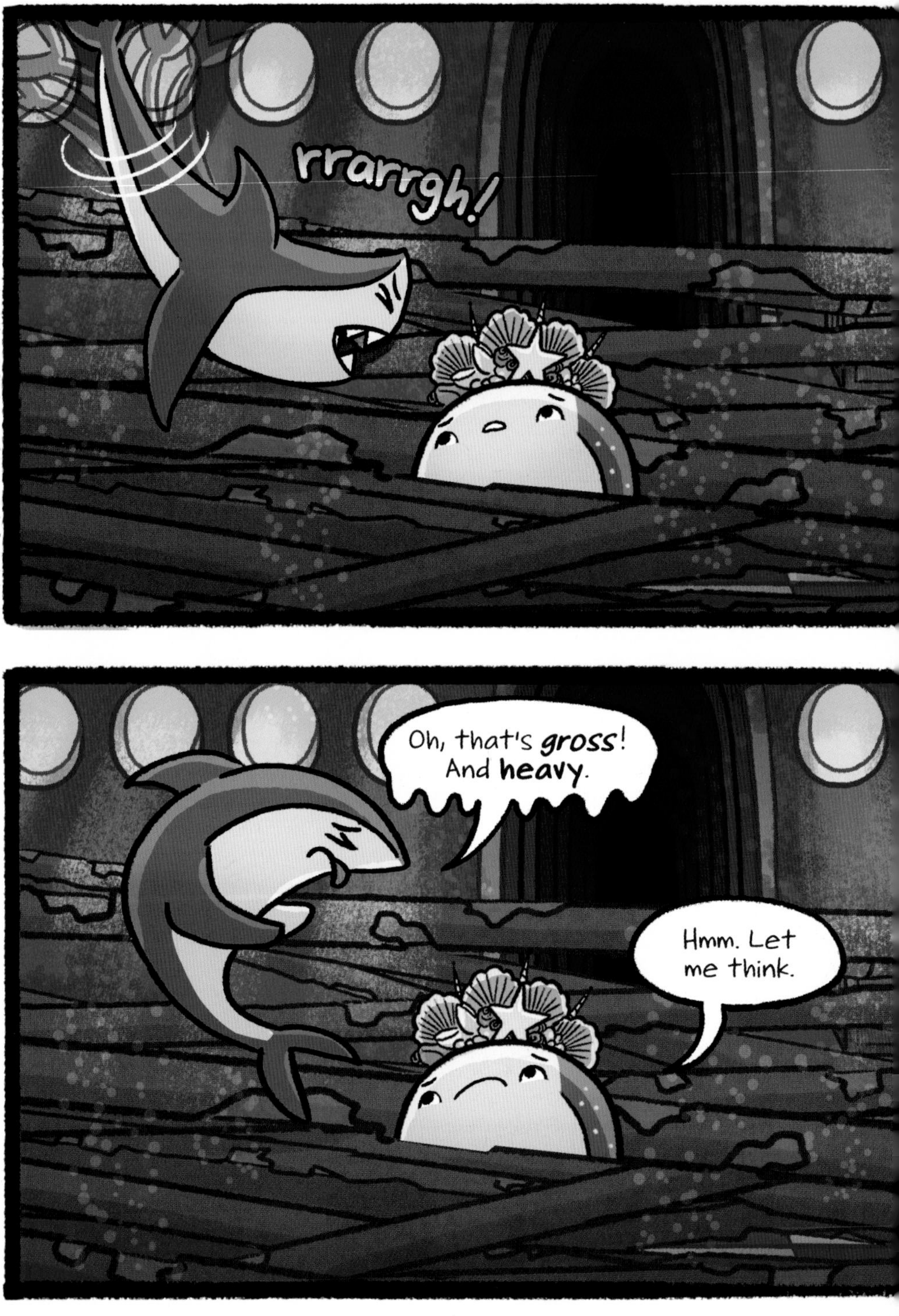
rrarrgh!
Oh, that's **gross**! And **heavy**.
Hmm. Let me think.

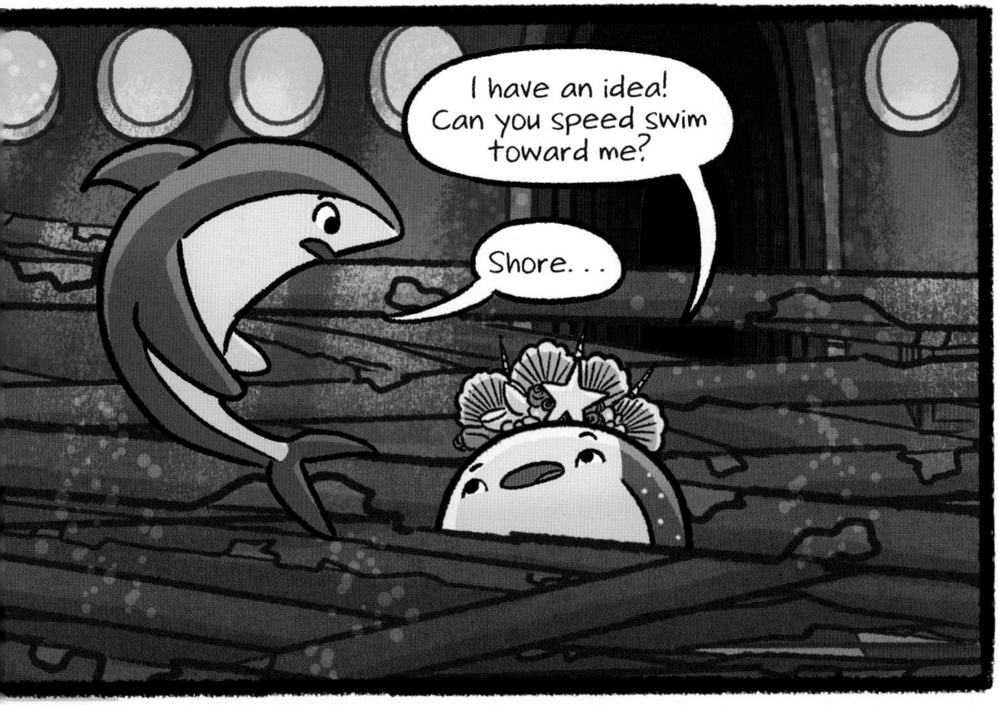
I have an idea! Can you speed swim toward me?
Shore. . .

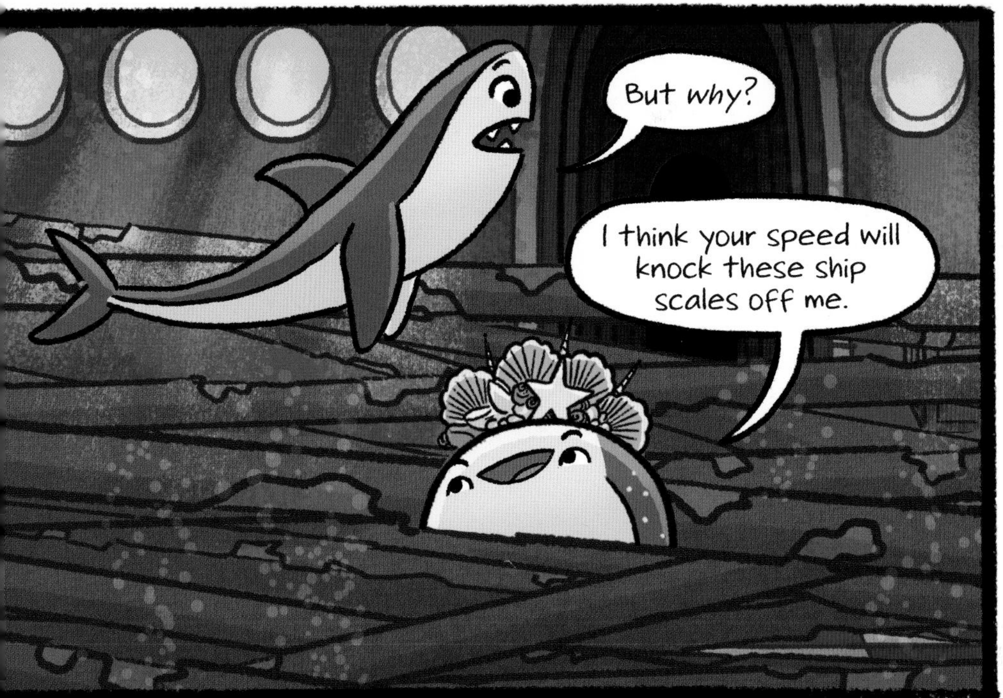
But why?
I think your speed will knock these ship scales off me.

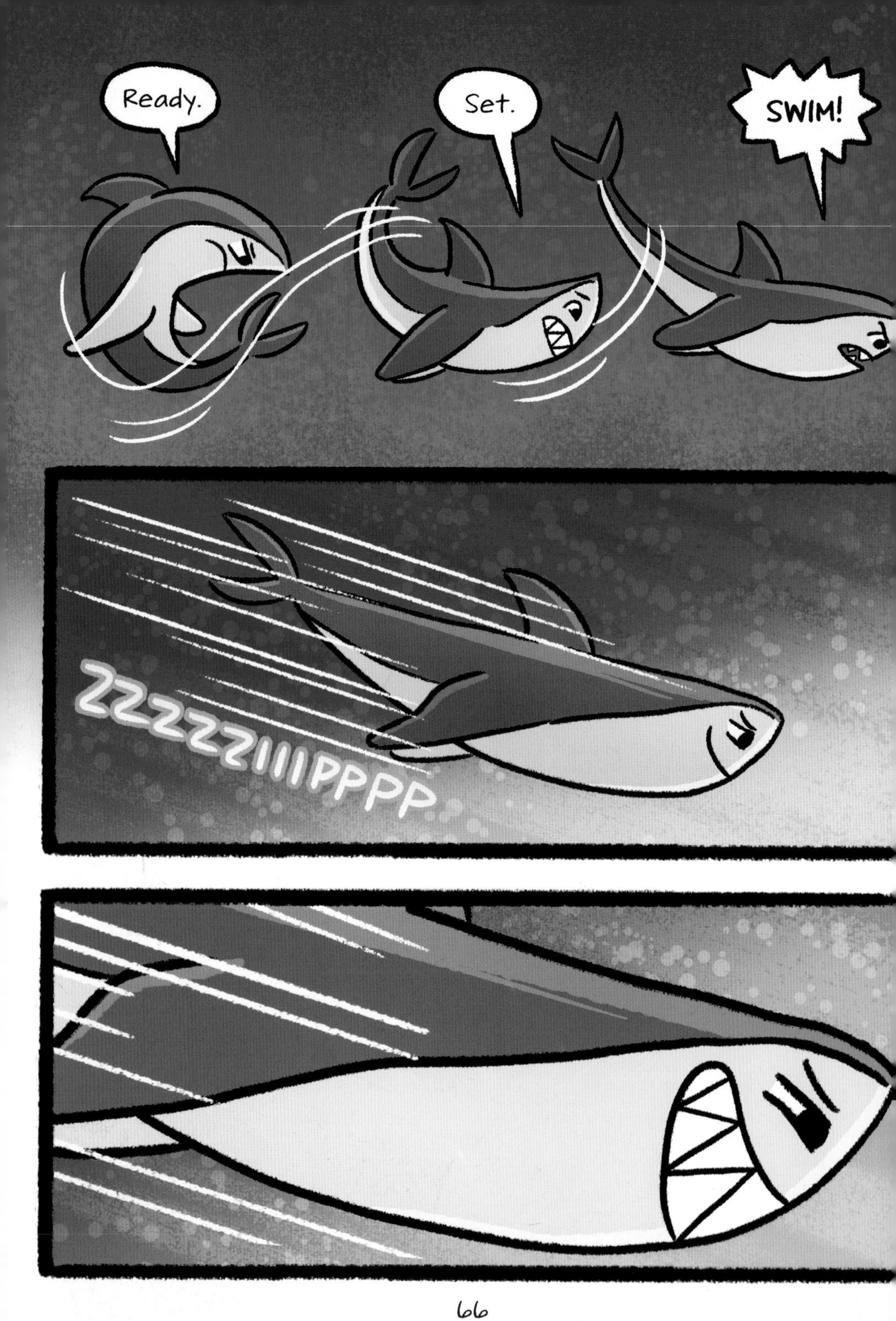
Ready.
Set.
SWIM!
ZZZZZZIIIPPPP

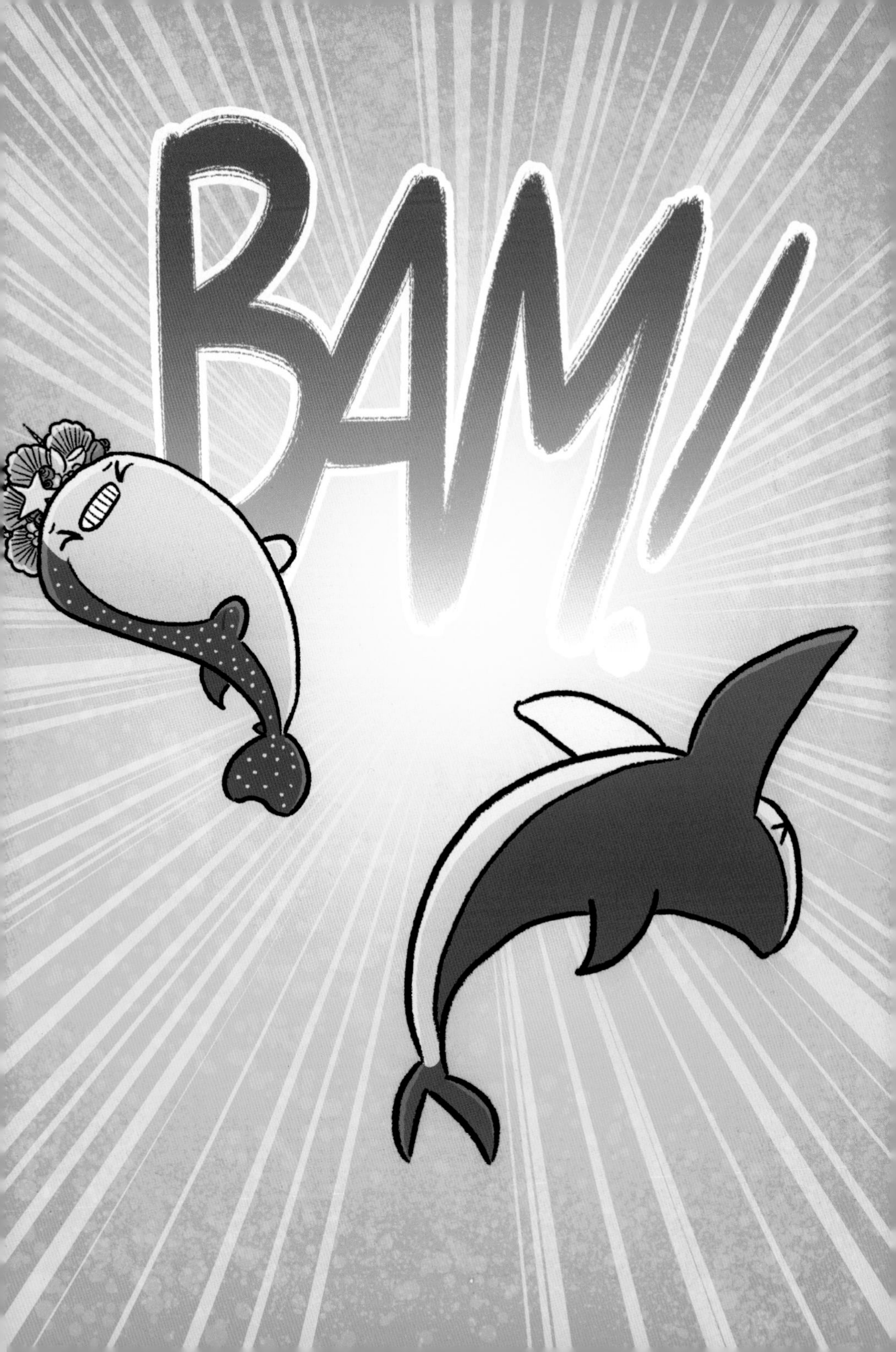
BAM!

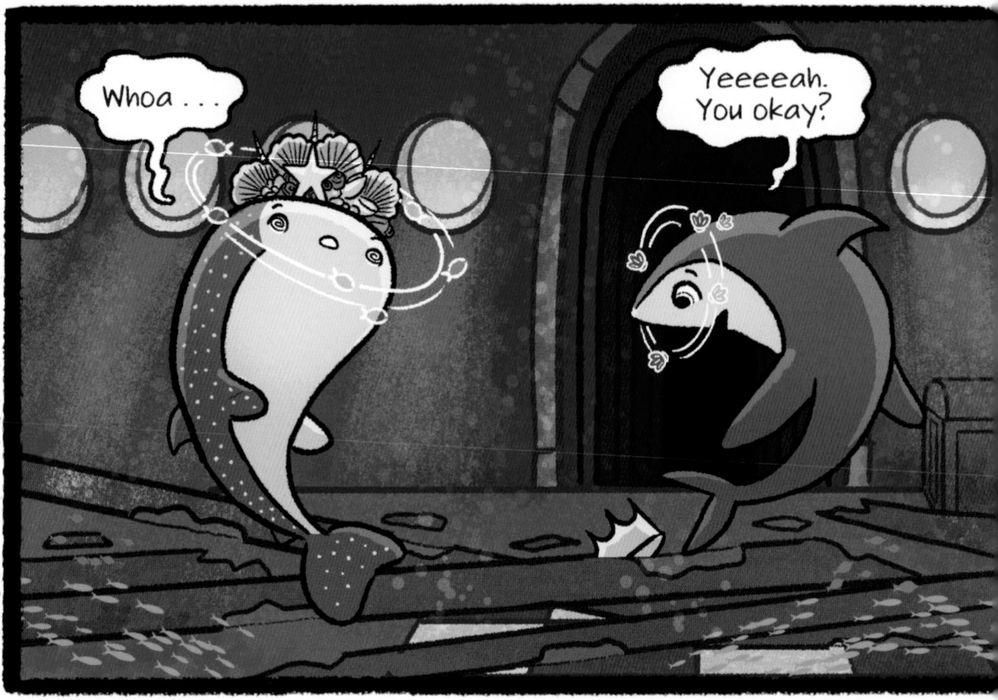
Whoa . . .
Yeeeeah. You okay?

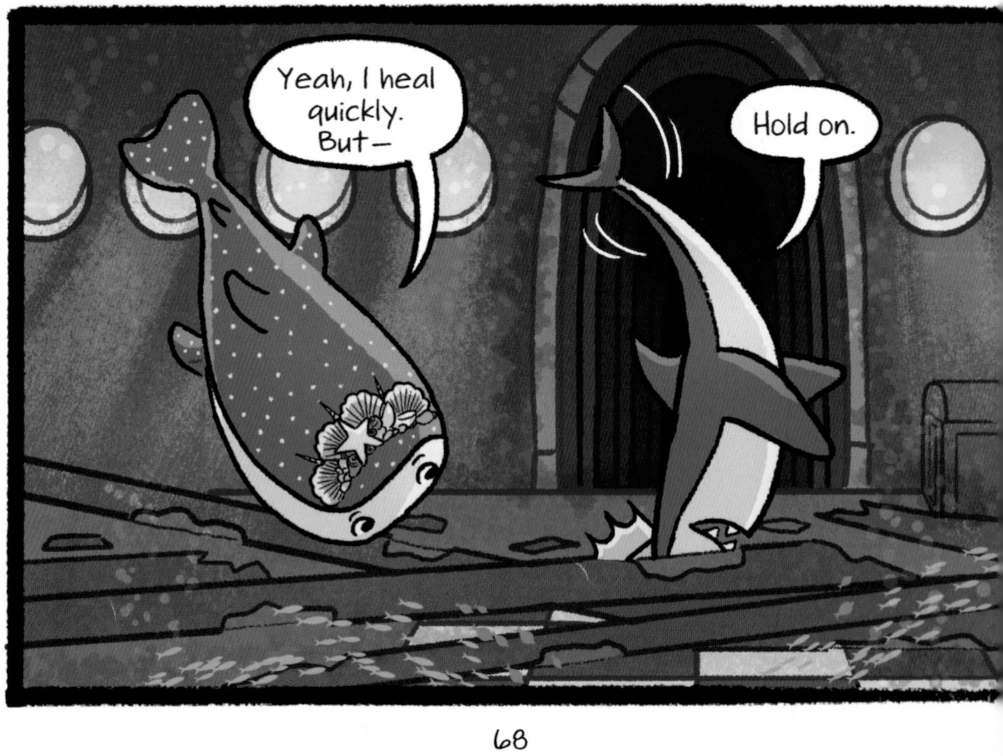
Yeah, I heal quickly. But—
Hold on.

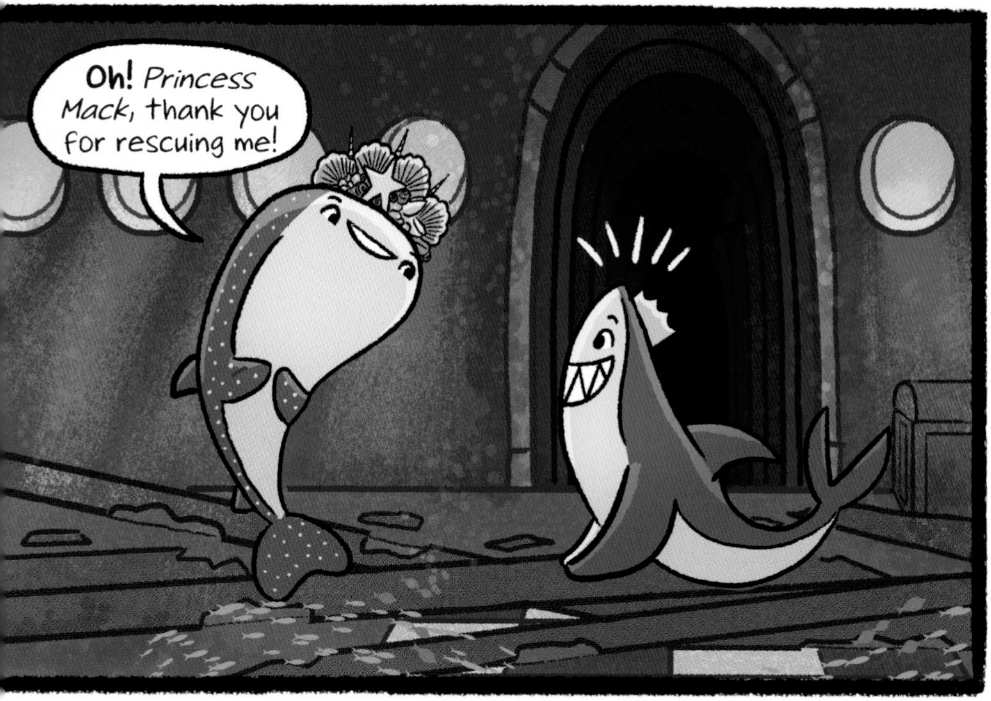
Oh! *Princess Mack, thank you for rescuing me!*

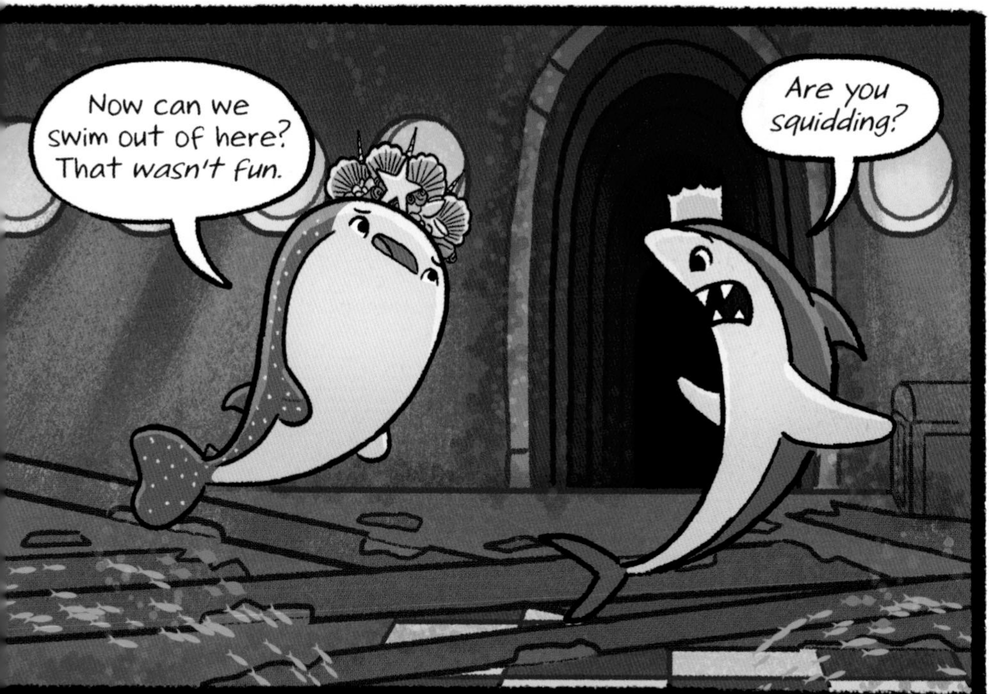
Now can we swim out of here? That *wasn't* fun.
Are you squidding?

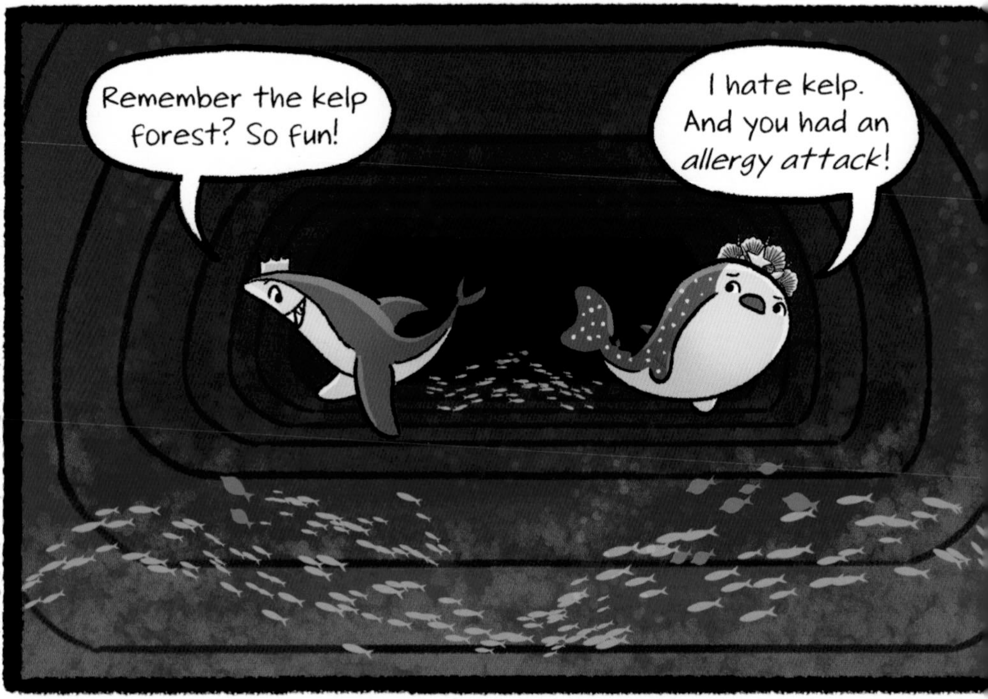
Remember the kelp forest? So fun!
I hate kelp. And you had an allergy attack!

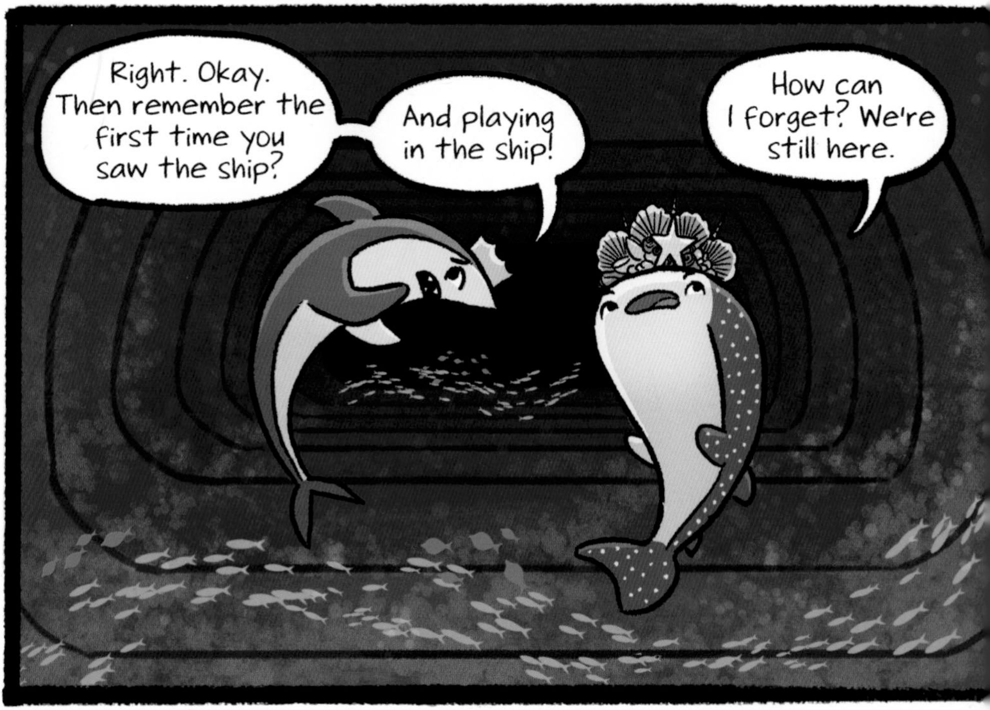
Right. Okay. Then remember the first time you saw the ship?
And playing in the ship!
How can I forget? We're still here.

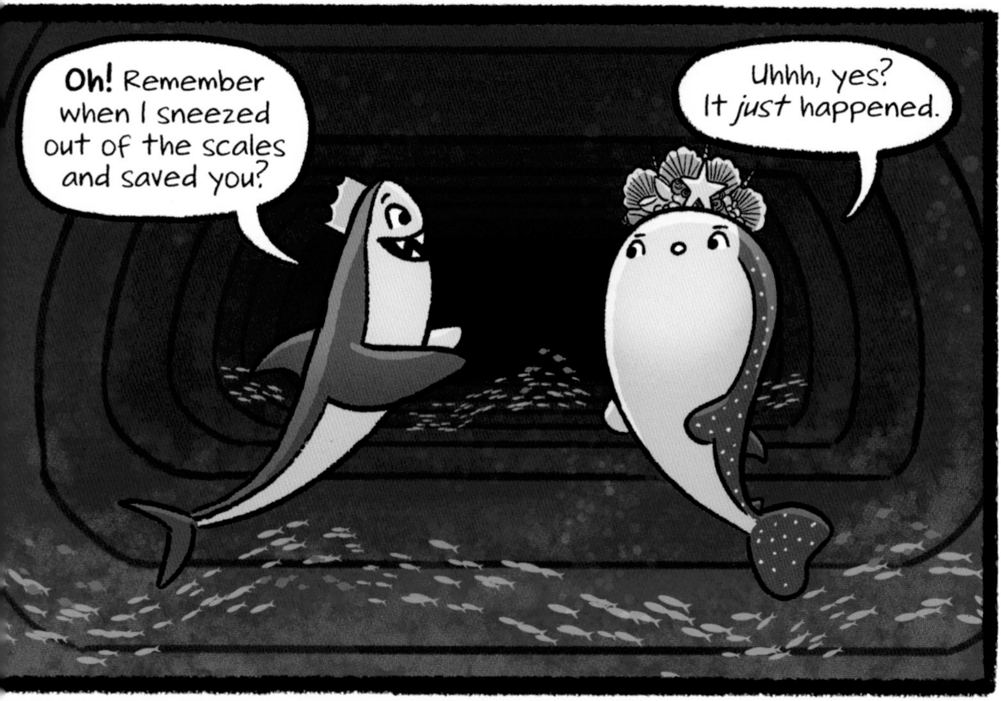
Oh! Remember when I sneezed out of the scales and saved you?
Uhhh, yes? It *just* happened.

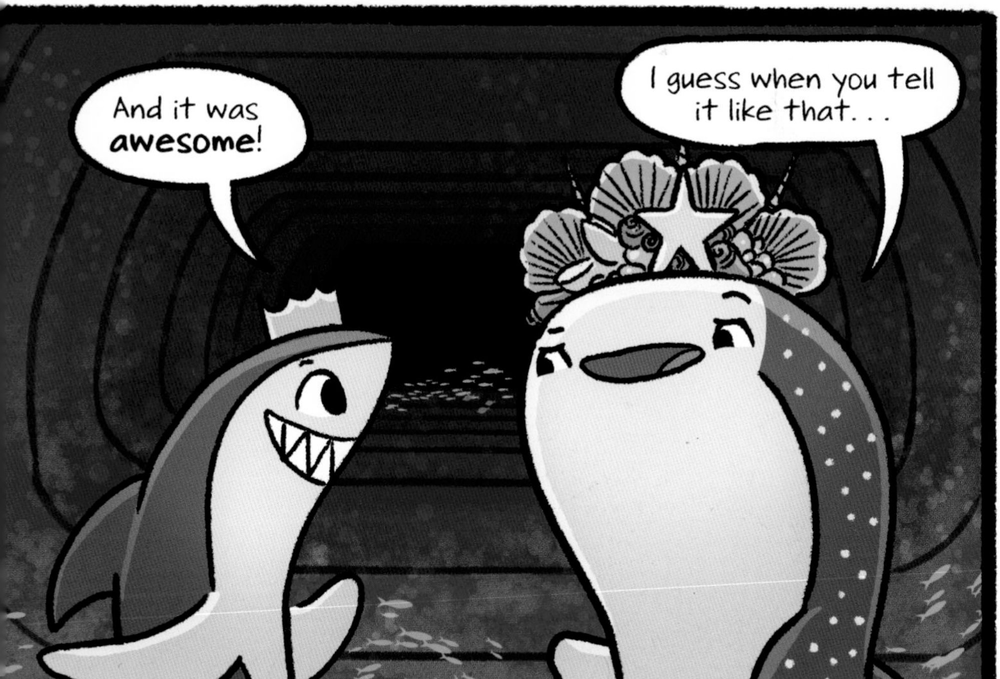
And it was **awesome**!
I guess when you tell it like that. . .

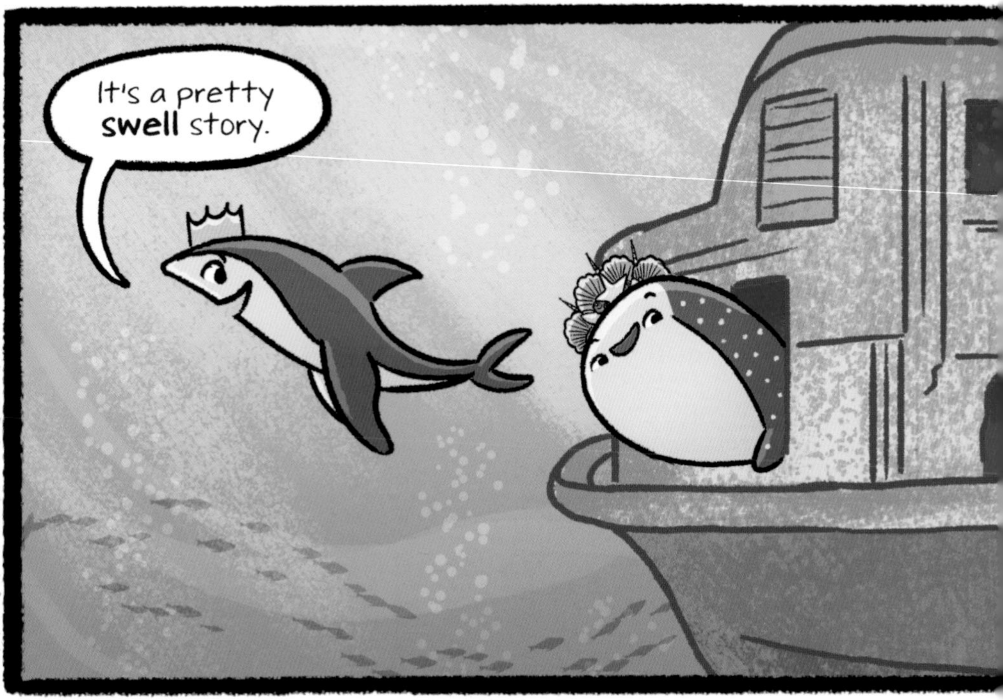
It's a pretty **swell** story.

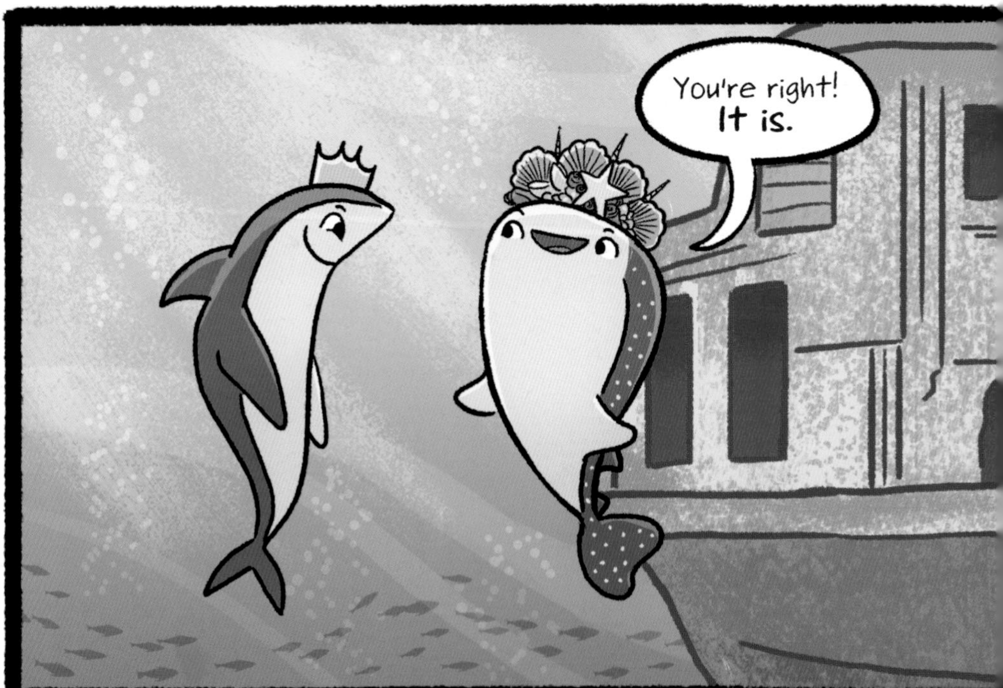
You're right! **It is.**

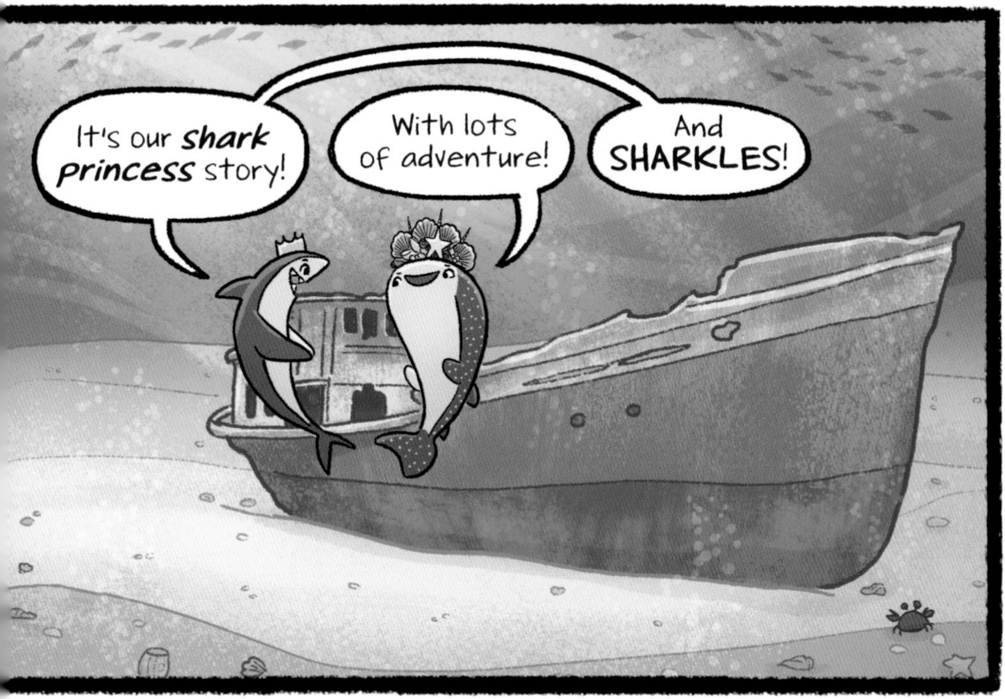
It's our **shark princess** story!
With lots of adventure!
And SHARKLES!

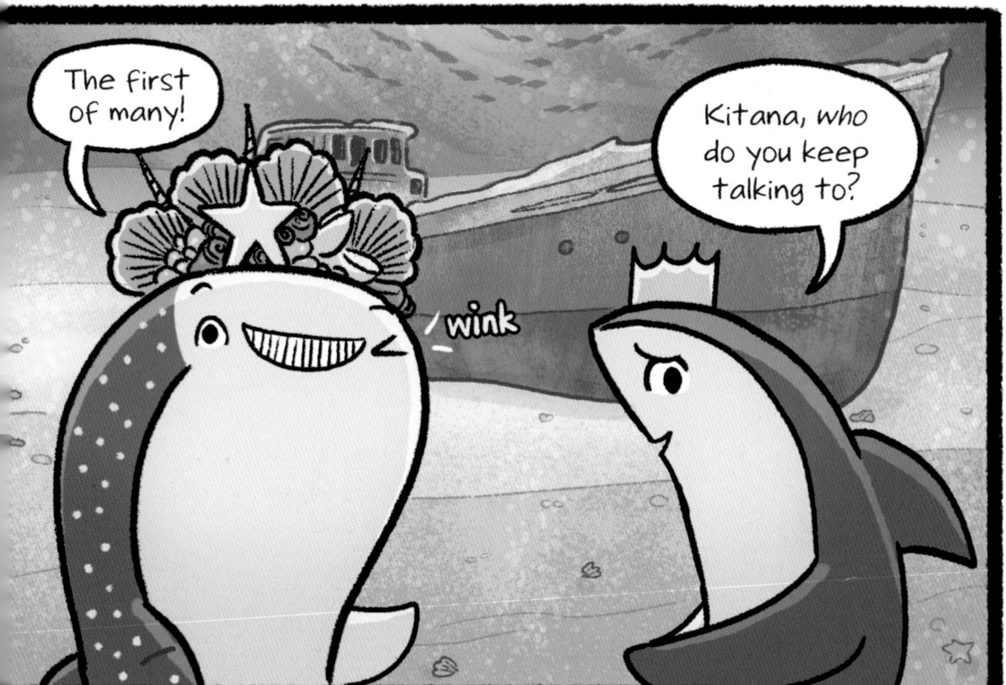
The first of many!
wink
Kitana, who do you keep talking to?

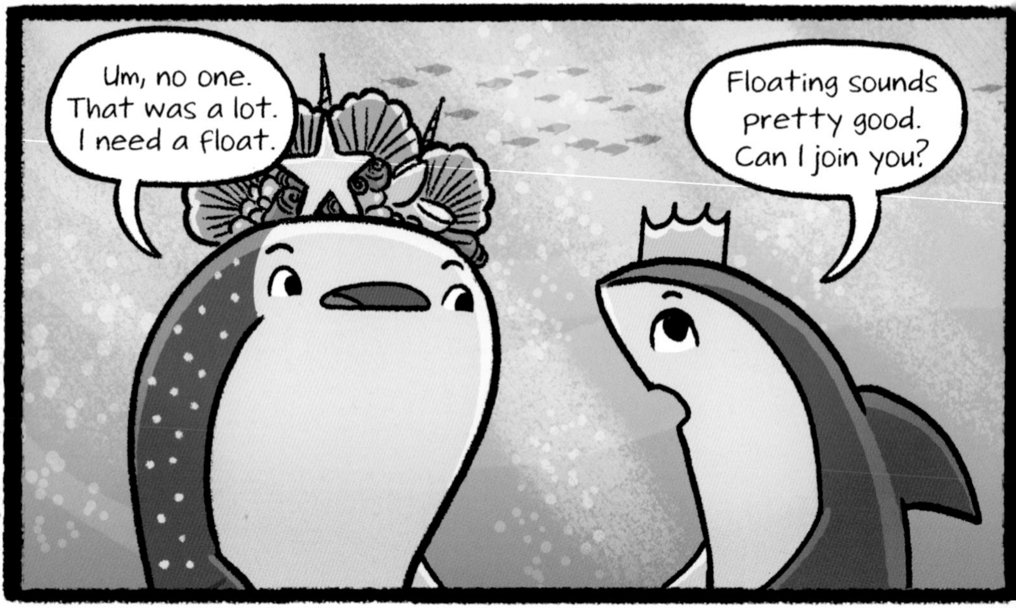
Um, no one. That was a lot. I need a float.
Floating sounds pretty good. Can I join you?

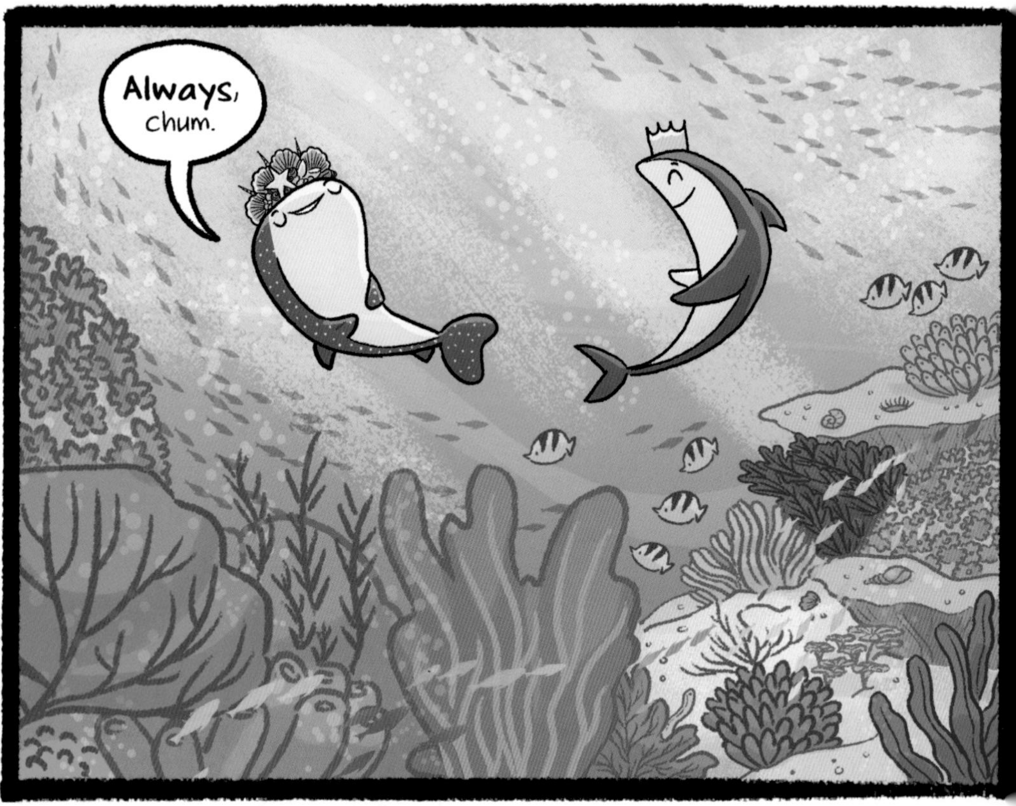
Always, chum.

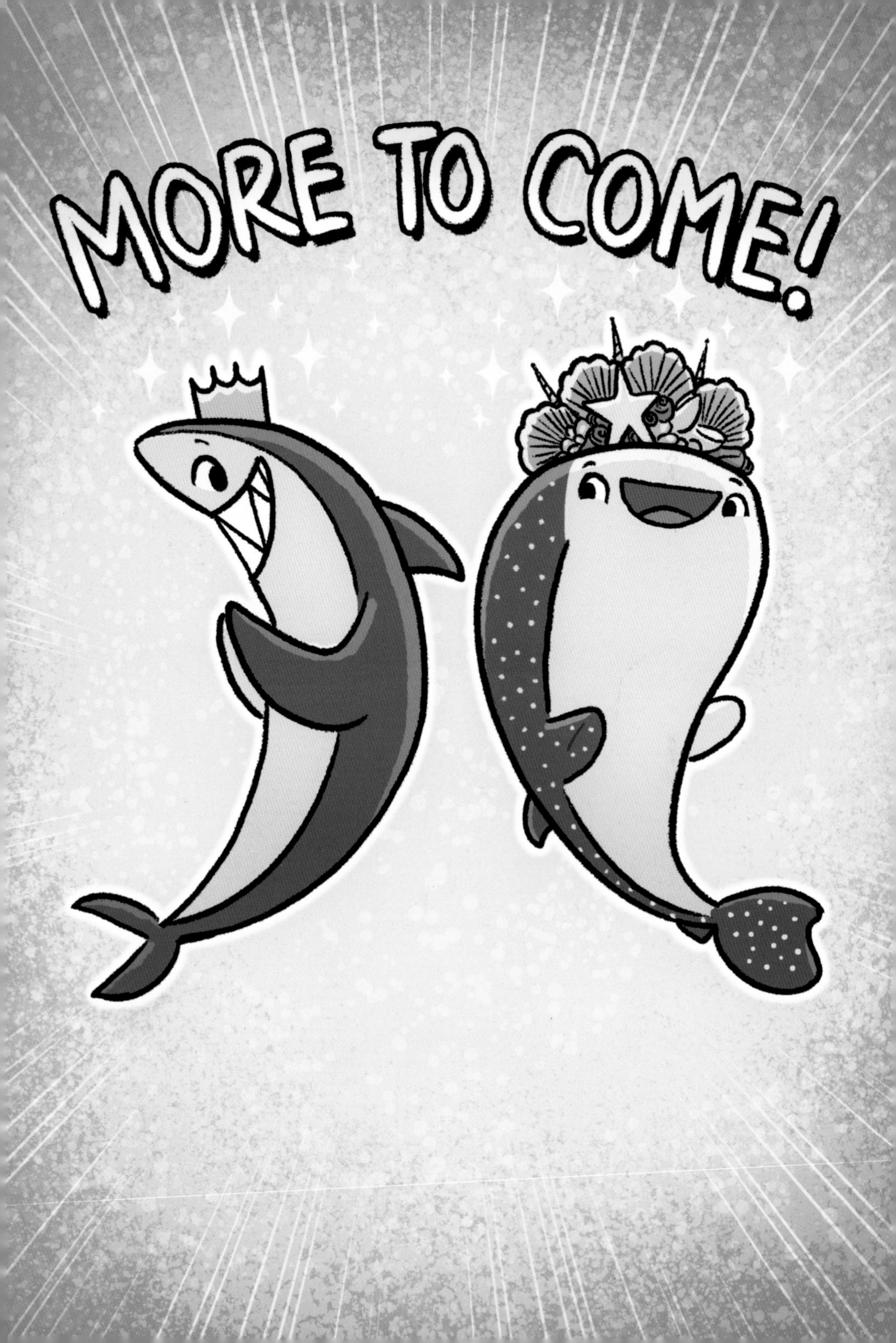
MORE TO COME!

HIDE AND SEA

Can you find all of the sea creatures
below in the pages of this book?

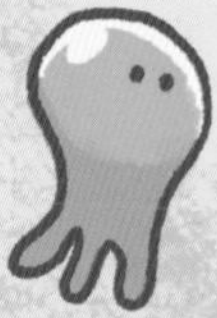

Reef
Octopus

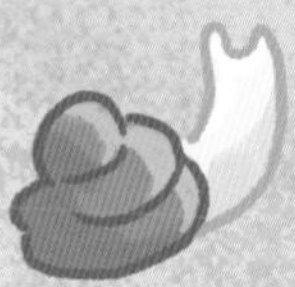

Periwinkle
Sea Snail

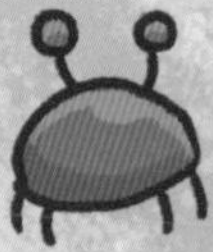

Ghost
Crab

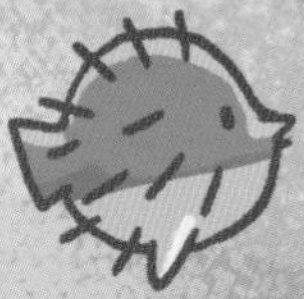

Puffer
Fish

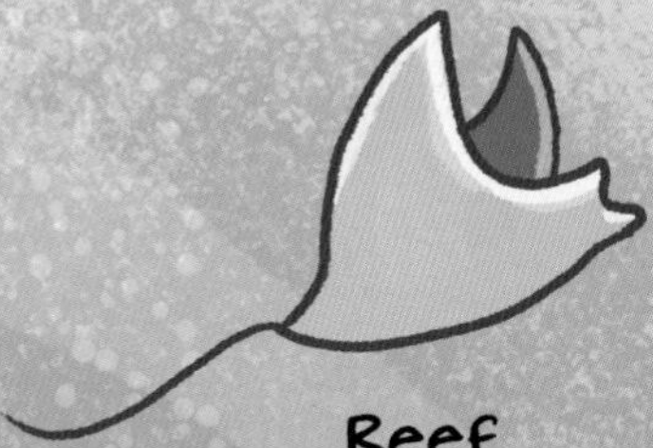

Reef
Manta Ray

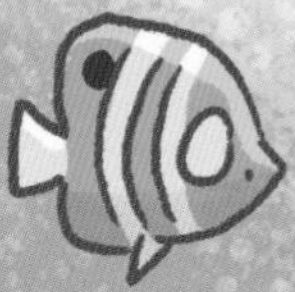

Butterfly
Fish

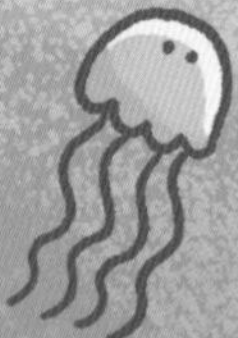

Blue
Jellyfish

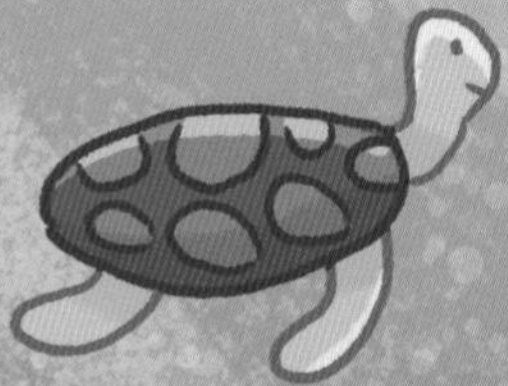

Green
Sea Turtle

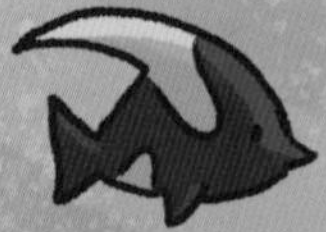

Angelfish

SHARK FACTS

WHALE SHARKS:
One of over 400 kinds of sharks!

Whale sharks are the **largest fish** on the planet

They can reach **46 feet** (14 meters) in length (longer than a school bus)

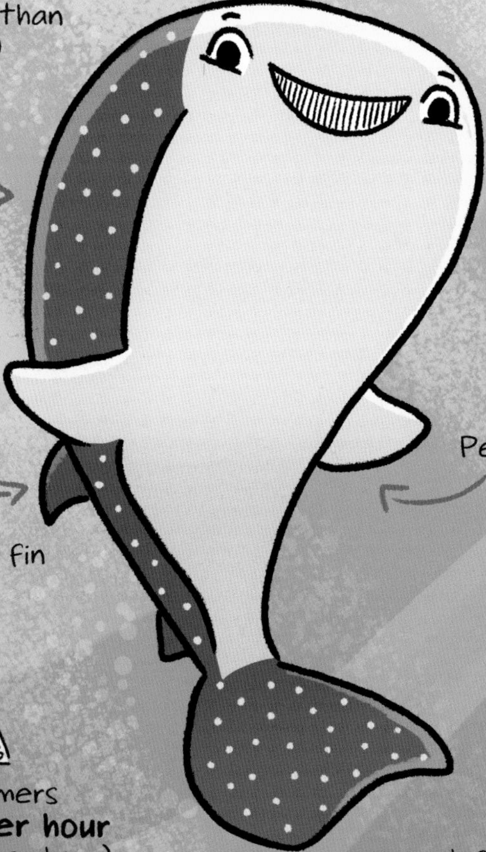

← **3,000** tiny teeth

White spots are **unique** to each whale shark, like a fingerprint

Pectoral fin

Dorsal fin

Slow swimmers at **3 miles per hour** (5 kilometers per hour)

Life span is from **100 to 150 years**

TREASURE TROVE

There are over 1 million shipwrecks undersea!

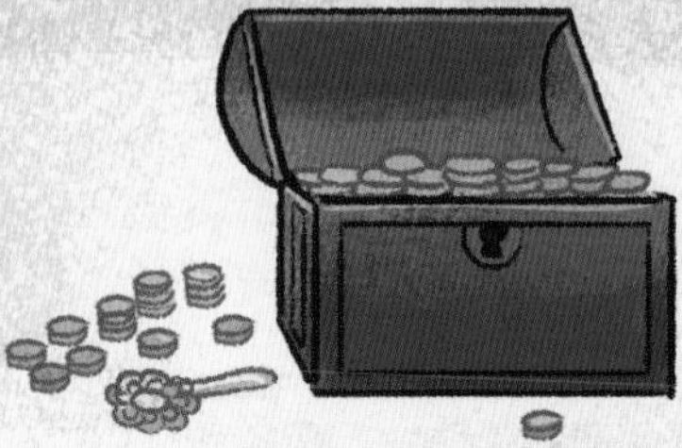

An estimated **$48 billion** worth of treasure is undersea

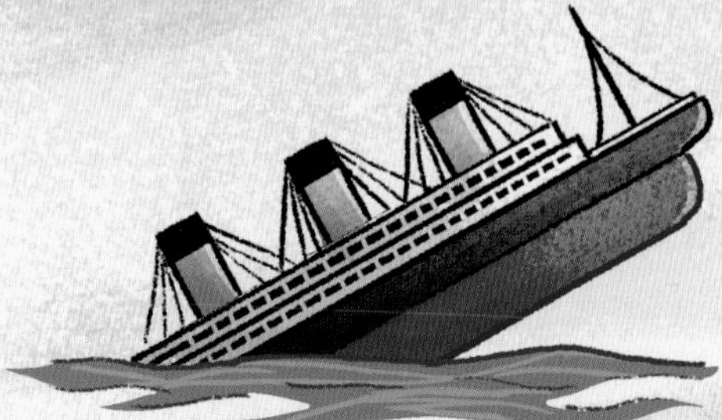

One of the most famous shipwrecks is the ***Titanic***

Flotsam
parts of a ship or cargo that floats on the ocean or washes onto land

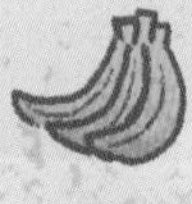

Unusual flotsam includes things like 1,000 bananas, dozens of fly swatters, and a BMW motorcycle

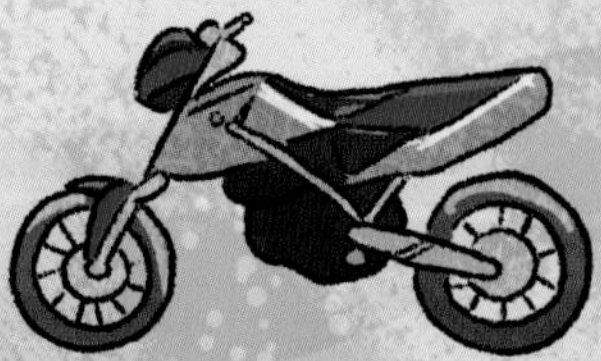

The oldest known shipwreck, the *Uluburun*, dates back to **1300 BC**

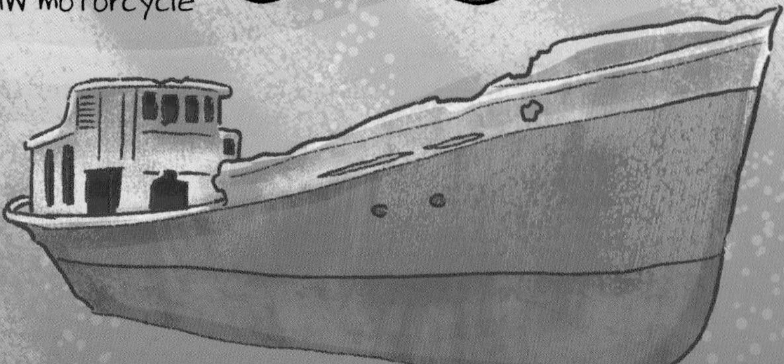

DRAW KITANA!

Learn how to draw the original SHARK PRINCESS!

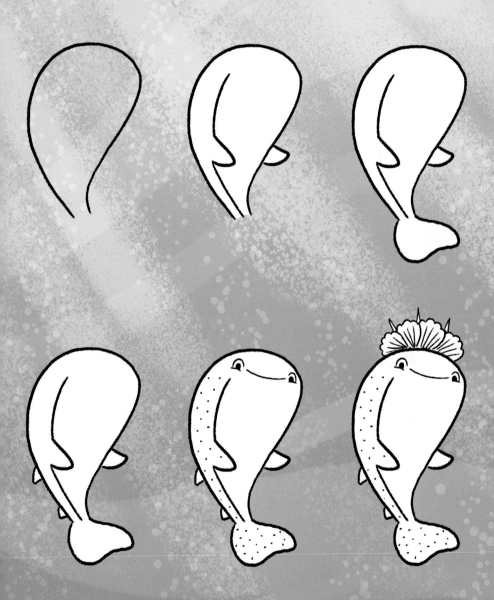

Nidhi Chanani spends her days drawing and her nights dreaming of snorkeling. She's the author of the graphic novels *Pashmina* and *Jukebox* and the picture book *What Will My Story Be?*, and the illustrator of many picture books, including *I Will Be Fierce*. Nidhi lives by the Pacific Ocean in the San Francisco Bay Area with her husband, daughter, and cats. Find more of her work at everydayloveart.com.